Hélène Grémillon was born in 1977 and lives in Paris. *The Confidant* is her first novel and has been translated from the original French into more than twenty languages.

Alison Anderson is a writer and translator. Her many translations from French include *The Elegance of the Hedgehog* by Muriel Barbery.

THE CONFIDANT

THE CONFIDANT

HÉLÈNE GRÉMILLON

TRANSLATED BY ALISON ANDERSON

Gallic Books
London

A Gallic Book

First published in France as *Le Confident* by Plon-JC Lattès, 2010
Copyright © Hélène Grémillon, 2010
English translation copyright © Alison Anderson, 2012

This edition published by Gallic Books, 2012
Gallic Books, 59 Ebury Street, London, SW1W 0NZ

Every reasonable effort has been made to contact copyright
holders and obtain the necessary permissions. In the event of
an inadvertent omission or error please notify the editorial
department at Gallic Books, at the address shown above, for
the correction to be made in future printings.

A CIP record for this book is available from the British Library
ISBN 978-1-908313-29-4

Typeset by Gallic Books in Book Antiqua and Helvetica
Printed and bound by CPI Group (UK) Ltd, Coydon, CR0 4YY

For Julien

The past wears
its armoured breastplate
and blocks its ears
with the wind's cotton wool.
No one will ever be able to
tear its secret away.

The Premonition
Federico García Lorca

Paris, 1975

I got a letter one day, a long letter that wasn't signed. This was quite an event, because I've never received much mail in my life. My letter box had never done anything more than inform me that the-sea-was-warm or that the-snow-was-good, so I didn't open it very often. Once a week, maybe twice in a gloomy week, when I hoped that a letter would change my life completely and utterly, like a telephone call can, or a trip on the métro, or closing my eyes and counting to ten before opening them again.

And then my mother died. And that was plenty, as far as changing my life went: your mother's death, you can't get much better than that.

I had never read any letters of condolence before. When my father died, my mother had spared me such funereal reading. All she did was show me the invitation to the awards ceremony for his medal. I can still remember that bloody ceremony, it was only three days after my thirteenth birthday. There was a tall

15

bloke shaking my hand, a smile on his face, but it was actually a grimace. His face was lopsided and when he spoke it was even worse.

'It is infinitely deplorable that death was the outcome of such an act of bravery. Mademoiselle, your father was a courageous man.'

'Is that what you say to all your war orphans? You think a feeling of pride will distract them from their sorrow? That's very charitable of you, but forget it, I don't feel sorrowful. And besides, my father was not a courageous man. Even the huge quantity of alcohol he consumed every day couldn't help him. So let's just say you've got the wrong man and leave it at that.'

'This may surprise you, Mademoiselle Werner, but I insist it is Sergeant Werner – your father – that I am talking about. He volunteered to lead the way, the field was mined and he knew it. Whether you like it or not, your father distinguished himself and you must accept this medal.'

'My father did not "distinguish himself", you stupid man with your lopsided face. He committed suicide and you have to tell my mother he did. I don't want to be the only one who knows, I want to be able to talk about it with her and with Pierre, too. You can't keep a father's suicide a secret.'

I often dream up conversations for myself, where I say what I am thinking; it's too late but it makes me feel better. In actual fact, I didn't go to the ceremony in honour of the veterans of the war in Indochina, and in actual fact I only ever said it once, other than in my own head – that my father had committed suicide – and that was to my mother, one Saturday, in the kitchen.

Saturday was the day we had chips and I was helping my mother peel the potatoes. It used to be Papa who helped her. He liked peeling and I liked to watch him. He was no more talkative when he was peeling than when he wasn't peeling, but at least there was a sound coming from him and that felt good. You know I love you, Camille. I always had the same words accompany every scrape of the knife as it sliced: you know I love you, Camille.

But that Saturday other words accompanied the scrape of my knife: 'Papa committed suicide, you knew that didn't you, Maman? That Papa committed suicide?' The frying pan fell, shattering the floor tiles, and the oil splattered onto my mother's rigid legs. Even though I cleaned frenetically for several days, our feet continued to stick, causing my words to grate in our ears: 'Papa committed suicide, you knew that didn't you, Maman? That Papa committed suicide?' To keep from hearing them, Pierre and I spoke more loudly – perhaps to mask Maman's silence as well, for she had hardly spoken at all since that Saturday.

The kitchen tiles are still broken. I was reminded last week while I was showing Maman's house to a couple who were interested. And if they turn into a buying couple, every time that interested couple looks at the big crack in the floor they will lament the prior owner's carelessness. The tiles will be the first thing they'll have to renovate, and they'll be pleased to get down to work. At least my horrible outburst will have been good for something. They absolutely must buy the house – whether it's this couple or another one makes no difference to me, but someone must buy it. I don't want it and neither does Pierre: a place where the slightest memory reminds you of the dead is not a place where you can live.

When she came back from the ceremony for Papa, Maman showed me the medal. She told me that the guy who had given it to her had a lopsided face and she tried to imitate him, tried to laugh. Ever since Papa died, that was all she could do: try. Then she gave me the medal, squeezing my hands very tight and telling me that it was mine by right, and she began to cry; that was something she could do without trying. Her tears fell on my hands, but I pulled away from her abruptly; I could not stand to feel my mother's pain in my body.

When I opened the first letters of condolence, my tears falling on my hands reminded me of Maman's, and I let them fall, to see where they might have gone, the tears of this woman I had loved so much. I knew what the letters would have to say: that Maman had been an extraordinary woman, that the loss of a loved one is a terrible thing, that nothing is more wrenching than bereavement, et cetera, et cetera, so I didn't need to read them. Every evening I divided the envelopes into two piles: on the right those with the sender's name on the envelope, and on the left those without. And all I did was open the pile on the left and jump immediately to the signature to see who had written to me and who I would have to thank. In the end I didn't thank a lot of people and nobody held it against me. Death forgives such lapses of courtesy.

*

The first letter from Louis was in the pile on the left. The envelope caught my attention even before I opened it: it was much thicker and heavier than the others. It was not the usual format for a letter of condolence.

It was handwritten, several pages long, unsigned.

Annie has always been a part of my life. I was two years old, just a few days short of my second birthday, when she was born. We lived in the same village – N. – and I often happened upon her when I wasn't looking for her – at school, out on walks, at church.

Mass was a terrible ordeal, for I invariably had to put up with the same routine, stuck between my father and mother. The pews one occupied at church reflected one's temperament: fraternal company for the gentler children among us, parental for the more recalcitrant. In this seating plan, which the entire village adopted by tacit consent, Annie was an exception, poor girl, for she was an only child, and I say 'poor girl' for she complained of it all the time. Her parents were already old when she came along, and her birth was hailed as such a miracle that not a day went by without them saying 'all three of us', in that way, whenever the opportunity arose, while Annie was sorry not to hear 'all four or five or six of us'…With every mass this unavoidable situation seemed to become all the more trying for her as she sat alone in her pew.

As for myself, while nowadays I hold boredom to be the best breeding ground for the imagination, in those days I had ordained that the best breeding ground for boredom was mass. I would never have thought that anything could happen to me at mass. Until that Sunday.

From the moment of the opening hymns a deep malaise came over me. Everything seemed off-balance – the altar, the organ, Christ on his cross.

'Stop breathing that way, Louis, everyone can hear you!'

My mother's scolding, added to the malaise that would not leave me, called to mind a phrase I had tucked away, words my father had murmured to her one evening: 'Old Fantin has breathed his last.'

My father was a doctor and he knew every expression there was for announcing a person's death. He used them one after the other, whispering into my mother's ear. But like all children I had a gift for picking up on what adults murmured to each other, and I had heard them all: 'close one's umbrella', 'die in his boots', 'give up the ghost', 'die a beautiful death' – I liked that last one, I imagined it did not hurt as much.

And what if I were dying?

After all, one never knows what dying is about until one dies for good.

And what if my next breath proved to be my last? Terrified, I held my breath and turned to the statue of Saint Roch, imploring him; he had cured the lepers, so surely he could save me.

*

21

It was out of the question for me to return to mass on the following Sunday; this time death would not pass me by, I was convinced of that. But when I found myself in the pew I occupied every week with my family, the malaise I was dreading did not descend upon me. On the contrary, I was overcome by a particularly sweet feeling, and I rediscovered with pleasure the smell of wood that was so peculiar to that church: everything was as it should be. My gaze was back where it belonged, focused on Annie, although all I could see of her was her hair.

Suddenly I understood that it was her absence the previous week that had thrown me into such horrible turmoil. She must have been lying down at home, with a facecloth on her forehead to calm her spasms, or she had been painting, protected from any abrupt movement. Annie was subject to violent fits of asthma, and we all envied her because this meant she was exempt from the activities we found unpleasant.

Her figure, still shaken by a slight cough, restored fullness and coherence to everything around me. She began to sing. She was not naturally joyful and I was always surprised to see her become animated and start singing so wholeheartedly the moment the organ sounded. I did not yet know that song was like laughter, and one could invest it with anything, even melancholy.

Most people fall in love with a person upon seeing them; in my case, love caught me off guard. Annie was not with me when she moved into my life. It was the year I turned twelve – she was two years younger, two years minus a few days. I began to love her the way a child does, that is, in the presence of other people. The thought of being alone with her did not occur to me, and I was not yet old enough for conversation. I loved her for love's sake, not in order to be loved. The mere fact of walking past Annie was enough to fill me with joy. I stole her ribbons so that she would run after me and snatch them, brusquely, from my hands before turning on her heels, brusquely. There is nothing more brusque than a little girl in a fit of pique. It was those scraps of cloth that she rearranged clumsily in her hair that made me think, for the first time, of the dolls in the shop.

My mother owned the village haberdashery. After school we both went there: I to join my mother and Annie to join hers, for Annie's mother spent half her life there, the half she did not spend sewing. One day, as Annie was walking past the shelf with the dolls I was suddenly struck by the resemblance. It was not only the ribbons; she had the same fierce white and fragile complexion as the dolls. At that point my youthful powers of reasoning got the better of me, and I realised that I had never seen any of her skin other than what her neck, face, feet, and hands could offer. Exactly like the porcelain dolls! Sometimes when I went through the waiting room at my father's surgery I would see Annie there. She always came alone to her consultations with my father, and she would sit there, so small in the black chair. When her asthma overwhelmed her she resembled the dolls more than ever, her coughing fit spreading like rouge over her cheeks.

But of course my father would never tell me that she had the body of a rag doll, even if I asked him about her. 'Professional secret,' he would reply, tapping me on the head before tapping Maman on the backside. And she would smile back at him with that smile I found so embarrassing.

As any resemblance is reciprocal, the porcelain dolls made me think of Annie. So I stole them. But once I was in the refuge of my room, I was inevitably struck by the fact that their hair was either too curly or too straight, their eyes too round or too green, and they never had Annie's long lashes that she curled with her index finger when she was thinking. These dolls were not meant to resemble anyone in particular, but I held it against them. So I went to the lake and tied a stone to their feet, then watched without sorrow as they sank effortlessly, my thoughts already on the new doll I would take and who would bear a greater resemblance to Annie, or so I hoped.

The lake was deep, and the spots where one could bathe without danger were rare indeed.

That year at the centre of the world there was me, and there was Annie. All around us lots of things were happening that I couldn't care less about. In Germany, Hitler had become chancellor of the Reich, and the Nazi party exercised single party rule. Brecht and Einstein had fled while Dachau was being built. It is the naïve pretension of childhood to think one can be sheltered from history.

I skimmed the letter, and had to go back and reread entire sentences. Since Maman's death I had no longer been able to concentrate on what I was reading: a manuscript I would normally have finished in one night now required several days.

It had to be a mistake. I did not know anyone called Louis or Annie. I turned the envelope over, but it was definitely my name and address. Someone else with the same surname, in all likelihood. The man called Louis would realise soon enough that he had made a mistake. I didn't dwell on it any longer and finished opening the other letters, which really were letters of condolence.

Like any good concierge, Madame Merleau had not been fooled by this flood of mail, and she handed me a little note: if need be, I must not hesitate, she was there.

I would miss Madame Merleau, more than I would miss my flat. The one I was moving into might be bigger, but I would never find a concierge as nice as she was. I didn't want to go through with this move. Couldn't I just stay in bed, here in this studio which scarcely a week ago I could hardly tolerate? I did not know where I would find the energy to drag all my stuff over to that place, but I no longer had the choice: I needed an extra room now. And besides, the papers had been signed and the deposit had been made; three months from now someone would be here in my place and I would be there in someone else's place, and they in turn would be in the place of…and so on. Over the telephone the man from the removal company had assured me it was true: if you followed every link of that chain, you invariably came back to yourself. I hung up. I couldn't care less about coming back to myself, all I wanted was to come back to my mother. Maman would have been happy to know I was moving; she had never liked this apartment, she only came here once. I never understood why, but that's the way she was, she took things to extremes sometimes.

Still, I had to let Madame Merleau know that I was moving out and thank her for her note.

'Oh, don't mention it, it's the least I can do.'

Whenever anything happens, a concierge already knows about it. She was clearly sorry for me, and she invited me to come in for a few minutes if I felt like talking. I didn't feel like talking, but I went in for a few minutes all the same. As a rule, we had always chatted at the window, never inside her loge. If I had not already known that this was a difficult moment for Madame Merleau, her invitation alone would have sufficed to make me understand. After she had closed the curtain behind us, she switched off the television and apologised.

'The moment I open that bloody window, people look inside. They can't help it. I don't think they're really curious, but it's unpleasant. Whereas when the television is on they hardly look at me. Fortunately the screen is enough to distract them. I couldn't stand to hear it blaring in my ears all day long.'

I felt ashamed and she realised.

'Forgive me, I wasn't saying that about you. You don't bother me.'

What a relief! I was off the hook – not part of the average mediocrity.

'With you it's not the same. You're nearsighted.'

I was startled.

'How did you know?'

'I know because nearsighted people have a particular way of looking. They always look at you more insistently. Because their eyes are not distracted by anything else.'

I was stunned. It was like being handicapped, with everyone pointing at you. Was it that obvious? Madame Merleau burst out laughing: 'I'm having you on. You told me yourself. Don't you remember, the day I told you about my fingers, you said it was sort of the same thing with your eyes. "Life is all about being dependent on your body's every little whim," that's what you said. I thought your explanation was terrifying and I remembered it, the way I remember everything I find terrifying. You have to always remember what you say and who you say it to, otherwise some day it might come back to haunt you.'

She leaned over to pour some coffee, but just then her hand began to shake with a violent tremor and the boiling liquid spilled onto my shoulder. I blew on the burn to cool it but above all so I would not have to look at Madame Merleau. I was terribly embarrassed to have witnessed her infirmity.

Before she became the concierge, Madame Merleau had been a tenant in the building. She arrived shortly after I did, two or three months, I think. The sound of her piano resounded throughout the building, but no one complained, her students were committed and the lessons never turned into an ordeal. On the contrary, the ongoing concert was quite pleasant. But as the weeks went by the piano was heard less and less, and I assumed that her students were getting married. Married people didn't take lessons any longer. Then the piano stopped altogether, and one day it was Madame Merleau herself who opened the window to the loge as I went by. She had acute rheumatism in her joints. The doctors conceded that it was an early onset, and that this sometimes happened, in particular with professional musicians, as their joints tired more quickly, by virtue of being called upon to play. They did not know exactly when, but eventually she would lose both the control and the mobility of her fingers; she was not to worry, she would still be able to use her hands for everyday things – eating, washing, brushing her hair, doing the housework – but she would no longer be able to use them for her profession, or at least not in all the subtle ways she had known up to now. In a matter of weeks she would lose the precious mastery that her hands had taken so many years to acquire.

She was completely devastated by the news. How would she live? The money from her lessons was her only source of income, she had no savings, and no one on whom she could rely, even for the time it would take to find her bearings. No parents, no children.

Then she heard that the concierge of the building was leaving. For several weeks people told her that she was the wrong age and didn't have the skills required for such a position. But she decided to submit her application to the owner, who agreed to give her the position. She bade farewell to her piano. She reasoned that an unfulfilled passion was too burdensome, and that one must know how to leave it behind in order to let another passion take its place. Why not astrology, for example? It would go well with her new profession as concierge, the know-all, gossipy side. And it would enable her to forestall her fits of clumsiness. If she had known she was going to spill the coffee today, she would not have offered me any. She smiled.

'You cannot go to work with your jumper in such a state. Go back upstairs and fetch another one. I'll take this one to the dry cleaner's, it will be ready this evening. I am really sorry.'

'Please don't bother, it's fine like this.'

'I insist.'

I wasn't one to insist so I went back upstairs. She could not be expected to know that I didn't have a single clean jumper in my wardrobe, that in fact I had nothing at all in my wardrobe, that all my clothes were on the floor and I walked all over them without caring. Just like Papa, I thought to myself, the moment I felt a bit of cloth underfoot: 'Pick them up, pick them up, please, you always pick up Papa's clothes, pick up mine, too!' But Maman did not pick them up. I managed to find one jacket that did not stink of cigarettes – it really was time to quit smoking.

Madame Merleau waved goodbye to me from the window. As the curtain fluttered closed I thought of how the last survivor of a family never receives any letters of condolence. With all that, I had completely forgotten to tell her that I was moving, but at least we didn't talk about Maman. Madame Merleau did not seem to be any more at ease in the realm of mourning than I was; so much the better.

That evening, when I came home, I was surprised not to find any letters in my box: the end of the letters of condolence already. Meagre takings, Maman. When I opened the door to my flat the smell of cleaning seized me by the throat: everything had been put away, the dishes I had not had the strength to wash for several days were now done, my laundry had been washed and ironed, and my sheets had been changed. A blinking light came from the door to the sitting room. Perhaps Maman's white ghost would smile at me the moment I entered the room.

The television had been left on, without the sound. Madame Merleau. Hanging in plain view from the wardrobe handle was my jumper, and she had left my letters on the table. A mixture of disappointment and gratitude overwhelmed me, and no doubt tears would have taken over, had my attention not been drawn to a letter that was bigger and thicker than the others. I opened it. Just as I thought. Him again. Louis was continuing his story where he had left off.

Annie and I attended the same school. Our institution was in a single building, but despite this apparent permissiveness, honour was intact, and the rules governing the division of the sexes were well and truly respected. The girls were on the ground floor, and the boys were upstairs. As a result of this chaste state of affairs, several days could drag by without my catching a glimpse of Annie, during which I was reduced simply to imagining her curling her eyelashes with her studious index finger, or to trying to guess which footsteps were hers when pupils went up to the blackboard, then moments of sudden delight when I recognised her cough.

I hated those two storeys. I hated them all the more given the fact that the arrangement had not always been like this. In the old days the girls used to be upstairs. My cousin Georges, for example, could still see the girls' panties as they came down the stairs four at a time – white ones, pink ones, blue ones, he filled his head with them as he gazed through the gaps in the stairway, all the better to admire the rainbow unfurling miraculously before him come rain or shine. But there we are; as is often the case, my generation had been sacrificed because of the idiocy of the previous one. Their lecherous ogling had not gone unobserved by Mademoiselle E., the headmistress, so the boys ended up on the upper floor, and without our shoes, which we had to take off so as not to make any noise. There we were for the girls to spy on in turn and make fun of the holes in our socks as we came down the stairs, shoving each other savagely to be the first out of doors. Because whoever was first out of doors was the winner; of course there was no reward, but at that age, the challenge itself was enough, particularly when the girls were watching. The number of bruises and falls that ensued must have worried Mademoiselle E., but she never went back on her decision, and morality continued to prevail over safety.

Until the blessed day when this despised arrangement ended up working in my favour. And why not, I too wanted to be the first out the door. It was a completely pointless resolution of mine, which landed me with a fractured shinbone and kept me immobilised for several weeks. But all was not lost and the point was revealed soon enough: the very next evening, Annie came to the door of my room. Given that she joined her mother at the haberdashery almost every evening anyway, Annie had volunteered to bring me my homework. She stood up, braving the sarcasm of the classroom and the idiotic guffaws that would designate her as the very girl I wanted her to be, 'my sweetheart'. She left me my lessons every day. Never before had I seen so much of her, and there I was, dazed, my leg stiff along with all the rest. I had to keep her there, longer than those few minutes she spent not knowing where to sit, and I not knowing where to look. We had both reached the age when our bodies had become important: hers was on display, and I could fantasise about it.

I was afraid that she might grow weary of this dull mission, that she might delegate someone else to perform it in her place. So under the pretext of an ordinary homework assignment, I asked my mother to borrow some books about painting from the library, and as I waited impatiently for Annie to make her appearance – fearing all the while that someone else would come – I immersed myself in reading. I hoped that by speaking to her of her passion I might, in turn, become an object of passion myself.

And that is how women painters became my new porcelain dolls, my new go-betweens in a love story for which I had not yet found the words. I told her about their lives in the most minute detail, and Annie listened attentively, without ever seeming surprised that I knew so much. I had succeeded: our minutes of conversation turned into hours.

That year, Tina Rossi sang 'Marinella', which I chanted alone in my room, as I staggered round on my broken leg. 'Annieeeella!' We were not the only ones putting on a show. In Germany, Hitler launched the Volkswagen 'Beetle' and violated the military clauses of the Treaty of Versailles. But as he could not be in two places at once, at the Berlin Olympic Games a black American was awarded four gold medals. In Spain, the civil war broke out, and at home in France, the Popular Front won the elections hands down.

I couldn't believe it, the correspondent still had it wrong. I had to find this guy and tell him he had the wrong addressee. But I had no way of tracing him, I couldn't send his letters back to him, there was no return address on the envelope. There wasn't even a signature; he did mention this 'Louis', granted, but 'Louis' who?

And were they even letters? They hardly looked like letters: no 'Mademoiselle' or 'Dear Camille' to start with. No indication of place or date on the letterhead. And to top it all off, the 'Louis' in question didn't even seem to be addressing anyone in particular.

I was startled by the sudden ringing of the phone. Who could be calling me in the middle of the night?

It was Pierre.

I hardly recognised my brother behind that faint, reedy voice asking me whether I realised we were now orphans? That word swept everything away. He couldn't sleep. I'd be right over. Could I stop and get him a pack of cigarettes? Of course.

This was not the time to lecture him. Besides, I felt like smoking, too, and I had thrown out what was to have been my last pack that very morning.

It is not other people who inflict the worst disappointments, but the shock between reality and the extravagance of our imagination.

Annie and I always walked together from school to the haberdashery. We never left at the same time, but the distance between us gradually shrank along the way. Whoever was walking in front would slow down, while the one behind picked up speed, until the two of us were walking side by side.

But years later, when we met again – on 4 October 1943, in Paris – Annie laughed and said I was the one who played both parts: either I caught up with her, or I let her catch up with me, but as far as she was concerned she swore she had never adjusted her speed. I did not seek to deny it; it was true that I wouldn't have missed those walks with her for the world. In my mind, I called them our 'lovers' strolls' – words often help to rearrange the nature of things. It was true, too, that I had long hoped for something between us, but things had turned out differently. She must have been married by then; at twenty, that was normal – I had deliberately aged her a year or two, to hurt her feelings a bit. I had seen the wedding ring on her finger. I was pretending. I was playing the part of the man who does not chase after women, who no longer hopes. The man whom one need not fear. As a child I had never used any tricks to secure her affections, but on that 4 October 1943, with my eyes glued to the ground to avoid her gaze, I could hear myself saying the exact opposite of what I was thinking. I was obligingly opening the way for her to tell me whatever she liked, with no regard for the past. What of her life, today? Was she happy?

Oddly enough, Annie replied with a confession.

'I must tell you, Louis, that you have always been the first. The first to kiss me, the first to caress my cheek, my breasts, the first who knew that there were days when I wore nothing under my skirt.'

Annie reminded me of all those first times; she remembered everything better than I did.

'Why did you never tell me this?'

She looked up at me.

'What's the point in telling a man that he was the first? Do you tell the twelfth man that he was the twelfth? Or the last that he was the last?'

I did not know what to say.

Did she hope, by pouring out all her memories, that I would forgive her for everything that never happened between us? The truth is, she began to change when she first started spending time with that Madame M.

Annie stood up abruptly, as if suddenly embarrassed to be near me. She offered me a chicory coffee, apologising that, because of the rationing, she no longer had any real coffee, or any sugar. She was nervous, opening all the cupboard doors as if she didn't really know what she was doing. Her apartment was very small. I watched her bare feet moving about her few square metres of living space. Her kitchen – a sink and a hot plate – was next to her bed, fortunately, for had she so much as left the room I might have doubted her very presence. I hadn't seen her for three years. For three years I'd had no news of her at all. At no time did I suspect she might be living in Paris like me. I looked at her fingernails, her peeling red varnish; in the village she never used to wear any. Seeing her again like this: it seemed too good to be true. Outside it was pitch black. I was suddenly overwhelmed by desire for her. She handed me a steaming hot cup.

'So, do you remember Monsieur and Madame M.?'

How could she ask me such a thing?

I rang the post office first thing next morning. The postmark indicated that the three letters had been mailed from the fifteenth arrondissement. Perhaps there was a number in the postmark that I had missed and that would indicate precisely which letter box had been used. I could go and put up a poster asking the famous Louis to contact me.

But their reply was unequivocal: there was no way to know. I couldn't exactly go putting posters on every letter box in the fifteenth arrondissement, I had plenty of other things to do, never mind the number of weirdos who would call me for all sorts of reasons, but never about the letters.

The letters had to mean something to someone, and somewhere in Paris there must have been another Camille Werner who was expecting them. She was the one I had to find. Sure at last that I had hit on the solution, I embarked on a search for all the homonyms. Shit! I would never have thought there could be so many Werners in Paris. I really have to stop swearing like this all the time, Pierre is right: it's not very feminine, it's hardly the way to make Nicolas come back to you. Shut up, Pierre. Don't talk to me about him. I don't go talking about the girls you sleep with, do I?

I called every Werner in the telephone directory to ask them 1) whether there was anyone by the name of Camille in their family, 2) did they by chance know anyone by the name of Annie? I met with a few polite, reserved 'no's. But some of the other reactions were quite surprising. There was one woman who hung up on me, terrified to hear an unfamiliar voice. There was one who didn't know any Annies, but she knew an Anna, was I sure I wasn't looking for an Anna? And then there was one who had scarcely had time to pick up the phone before her husband started shouting at her to hang up, telling her it was robbers, that's what they always do in the holidays, to find out whether anyone was at home.

But no sign anywhere of another Camille Werner.

Tough luck, Louis. He would have to go on writing to me for no good reason.

By Tuesday a new envelope was waiting for me, just as thick, but all alone now in my letter box. The same stationery, a very smooth parchment; the same handwriting – a distinctive capital 'ʀ', the same size as a lowercase letter, slipping effortlessly into the heart of a word – and the same smoky scent, a perfume that reminded me of something or someone, but I couldn't figure out who or what.

Monsieur and Madame M. were a very wealthy young couple. Both sets of their parents had flawlessly fulfilled their duty as overzealous forebears by dying unusually young and unusually rich. Their last will and testament was dripping with real estate, but the M. couple chose to settle in L'Escalier, to our great misfortune.

L'Escalier was the name given to a fine estate in the middle of our little village, as out of place as a swan among starlings. Children thought of it as a haunted manor house; young people as a romantic château, and those who had reached an age where one's sole entertainment was the misfortune of others viewed it as a potential source of iniquitous family disputes: consequently, L'Escalier belonged more to the collective unconscious than to any ordinary owner. When the M. couple moved in, it was like a violation, and everyone felt dispossessed by the intrusion of these strangers. Everyone except Annie, who was looking forward to an opportunity for new paintings. She had already painted the estate from every angle the high stone wall would allow, and although the wall had crumbled here and there, it nevertheless did continue, like some old guard dog, to dissuade any intruders.

One morning two servants – a man and a woman – arrived with a load of baggage and furniture. Luxury items were part of the journey; this was a major move. The trunks were overflowing with carpets, paintings, chandeliers and all sorts of artefacts.

'They're cleaning the house from top to bottom, they've piled everything in the courtyard, come and see, it will make a nice painting.'

I had followed Annie to the elm tree where she was in the habit of sitting. She liked to show me her canvases, to see what I thought of them. Her painting was rather good. She had captured perfectly every trace of the sudden agitation at the house – the shutters flung open, the dust blowing out of the windows, the grounds as they were cleared and began to look like proper grounds again. Annie was quite pleased, except for her portrayal of the man.

'I've made a mess of him – he walks with a limp but in the picture you can't tell. I can't paint anyway, so when he's a cripple, it's even harder.'

I pointed out to her that it must be a family who were moving in. She asked me why I thought so. I pointed to the crib and the pram on her canvas. Strangely enough, although she had painted them, she hadn't seen them. Can human beings sense danger to a point where they deny it? Annie was absorbed in a silent reverie. I could tell as much, her brush was already circling round a child caught in its mother's skirts.

*

When I try to understand the reasons behind the whole tragedy, I always come to the same conclusion: if Annie had not been passionate about painting, none of this would ever have happened. I am as certain of this as are those who maintain that if Hitler had not failed his entrance exam to art school the world would have been a better place. The young girl painting caught Madame M.'s eye, and that is why she invited her to come in for a few minutes, the time it took for a cup of tea. Otherwise they would never have met; they would have remained mutual strangers kept apart by everything since birth.

Some people said, 'Madame M. is bored all on her own'; others added, 'and she is still so young'. The entire village tried to find an explanation for this unnatural friendship between a *bourgeoise* from a high-ranking family and their little Annie. After they had rejected the excuse – too humiliating – that 'rich people like the poor when they are nice-looking', they finally opted for the commonsense explanation that 'rich people like artists', and I think they were right.

Everyone got used to them spending time together, and were even rather proud of them. Everyone, that is, except me. I took a dim view of their friendship. Annie, who was anti-social by nature, seemed to have found in that young woman the type of person one meets only once in a lifetime: the one who can replace everyone else. Once she had got into the habit of stopping off for tea with Madame M., Annie gave up all her other habits, including me. She cut herself off from my life, or rather, she cut me out of her life, without the slightest compunction, and without giving me any explanation as to her sudden detachment. She did not ignore me, what she did was worse: she still greeted me with that horrible little wave that was proof she had seen me, but never again with the other wave that was an invitation to join her. Love is a mysterious principle, falling out of love more mysterious still, and one can know why one loves but never, truly, why one has ceased to love.

Things could have stopped there, I could certainly have swallowed my gnawing irritation, my jealous resentment, but the arrival of Monsieur and Madame M. in L'Escalier was about to turn into an irreversible tragedy.

So did I remember them?

'Annie, you might as well have asked me if I remembered that we had lost the war.'

Visibly feverish, she did not stop stirring the spoon in her cup. 'Don't compare things that cannot be compared.' Annie slowly hitched her cardigan onto her shoulders. I could not take my eyes off her; her eyes were riveted elsewhere. I sensed that it was not only our 'first times' that she had to tell me about. She had simply reminded me of those times in order to earn the right to tell me what really mattered, the way one forces oneself to inquire politely about one's interlocutor before launching into a monologue where one speaks only of oneself.

'I have something to confess, Louis. I have to tell you what really happened with Monsieur and Madame M. You are the only person I can tell.'

That letter stopped there; I was going to have to wait to find out what happened next.

It was precisely the suspense that got me thinking and made me reread it from another point of view, that of my profession as an editor this time. There was something literary about it, and now that I had noticed it, the same was true about the earlier letters. What an idiot I was not to have realised sooner! My mother's death must have really made me lose my grip. Those letters were meant for me, all right: it was simply an author sending me his manuscript through the letters. I received too many manuscripts to read all of them, they piled up on my desk, and authors were aware of this, particularly the unpublished ones. That was why these letters didn't really follow a traditional format; they were instalments of a book that I'd be receiving week after week. A crazy idea, but not stupid. The proof: I was reading them.

I started observing my authors closely, trying to trap them by insinuating this or that, hoping one of them

46

would betray himself; they must have thought I was going mad. I would study their handwriting, searching for that capital 'ʀ' in the middle of all the lowercase letters. I would take a close sniff, ever on the lookout for that woody perfume that came from the letters. I entertained every possibility. Could it be So-and-so? That would be just like him to write a thing about his childhood. It was becoming increasingly common to write about oneself, so if that was it, I would give it to him, straight to his face: that I was expecting a novel from him, a real one. I would aim for his glasses: it would be great if they fell off, I've always wondered what he'd look like without his glasses.

I was convinced the sender of the letters would show up at my desk one day. A stranger would ask to see me, and bring me the rest of his manuscript, apologising for having duped me, but hey, for fifty years he'd never duped a soul and for fifty years no one had paid him the slightest attention, so he'd decided to change tack.

And what if it were the little Mélanie? 'Have any of your interns ever become one of your authors?' If she thought I didn't notice what she was driving at with all her questions…But no, it was impossible, she was too young, these letters were the work of someone older, you could tell, and besides she was too pretty to write like that.

It was Mélanie, in fact, who roused me from my thoughts, one hand on the microphone of the receiver to keep Nicolas, on the other end of the line, from hearing her:

'Your friend insists on speaking to you.'

'Tell him I'm in a meeting.'

'I did, but he's already called five times this morning, he said he knows you're not in a meeting.'

'If he doesn't want me to be in a meeting, then tell him I don't want to talk to him. People won't let go if you lie to them, but they will if you tell them the truth.'

And if I told him the whole truth, I'll bet you anything the guy would let go in no time; he'd probably run for his life.

At any rate I could not go on like that, it was too risky. I decided to go home early, especially as I was sure of finding something in my letter box. It was Tuesday, and I'd noticed the letters always arrived on a Tuesday; my correspondent had the idiosyncrasies of a serial killer.

In those days I still found the letters entertaining, almost friendly – a touch of mystery, in a world that was completely devoid of it, was hardly unpleasant. And besides, I wanted to find out what happened, what was this terrible tragedy involving Monsieur and Madame M.?

Not for one second could I imagine what was coming. The unthinkable does exist: I'm proof of it.

I went to their house nearly every day. I would paint while Madame M. read to me out loud. It was pleasant; she played all the characters. I enjoyed her company. I didn't even feel obliged to speak, something that had never happened to me with anyone. She was so generous with me.

She had put an entire room at my disposal. 'The room without walls.' That was what she called it because the walls disappeared behind a huge mirror and some heavy red drapes. It was too beautiful to be converted into a studio, but she would not have it any other way. 'My dear Annie, since I have already told you how much pleasure it gives me...' And it was the same with all the rest. I asked for nothing, she gave me whatever I needed. When I had finished a canvas, a new one would appear as if by magic. She thought of everything. She even asked a friend of hers to give me lessons: Alberto, a marvellous painter and sculptor. He came from Paris, every Thursday. She was so kind.

I had certainly noticed that she wasn't happy, but I

had not managed to find out why. As far as I could tell she had all the best things life has to offer.

In the beginning I thought she must be ill. It was Sophie, their maid, who put this idea into my head. One morning I had not dared go into L'Escalier, there was a car parked in the drive and I thought this might be 'her new infatuation'. My papa was forever telling me I must not have any illusions, that Madame M. and I did not belong in the same world, that she would replace me soon enough, just you wait. I retraced my steps and went home again. But two hours later Sophie was knocking on our door to ask for news; Madame M. was concerned I might be ill. I told Sophie about the car, and she replied that I was being silly, that I was always welcome at L'Escalier, that since she had met me Madame was improving by the day. Her words worried me. So I asked her if Madame M. was ill. She helped me on with my coat; No, what she meant was that Madame was happy to have me there with her, whether there was a car parked in the drive or not. I could sense she wasn't telling the truth.

Roughly two weeks later I had further proof that something was not quite right. This time it was her husband's car that was parked in the drive. As a rule he had already left for his newspaper office by the time I arrived. I didn't really feel like meeting him, but I couldn't just turn around, Madame M. would have thought I was being ridiculous with my scrupulous politeness. She had made me promise I would never again hesitate to come in. So in I went, but I soon regretted it, for they were in the midst of an argument.

'This cannot go on! If I agreed to come and live here, it was so you would feel better, not so you would go on feeling sorry for yourself.'

'I am not feeling sorry for myself.'

'I no longer recognise you. It is not by shutting yourself off from the rest of the world that you are going to solve your problem.'

'May I point out that it is also your problem.'

'No. My only problem is that I come back here every night and find my wife no longer has a care in the world other than to make sure that I have bought canvases or charcoal or acrylic for her...I cannot believe you have no idea what is going on in the world, honestly! You are worse than the women you are avoiding.'

'I'm not avoiding anyone.'

'What's the use of trying to talk to you, and anyway, now I'm late...'

'That's it! Leave! Go back to your wonderful world where everyone knows everything that's going on...Go and tell your beloved readers what makes the world go round, and above all don't bother to explain anything to me, to explain how our world is supposed to go on working with everything that's happened to us.'

Her husband left the drawing room without replying. He looked upset, he even walked right past me, thinking I was Sophie: 'Don't you have anything to do in this house?' Madame M. had rushed out behind him. She watched him leave, murmuring something I did not manage to hear. When she turned round, we were face to face. 'What are you doing here, eavesdropping like that?' She had never spoken to me in this way. I did not try to defend myself, and I left. But she ran after me.

She was so sorry, she should not have allowed herself to get carried away, it was not my fault, she did not want me to leave. She had hurt me, and I accepted her apology. I shouldn't have.

As is sometimes the case with arguments, this one brought us closer together. We began to speak more often after that. Madame M. stopped reading her novels, no doubt because of her husband's reproaches. 'There is no place for fiction in these turbulent times, to have your nose in a book is to have your back to the enemy,' she would say, imitating her husband's voice. I asked her to go on reading out loud, even if it was only newspapers. That was how our conversations began, as we talked about the articles. We were surprised, we got along well. There were nearly ten years between us, but we didn't really feel it. She had never befriended anyone as young as me. She said it was her wealth that had kept her apart from her generation. In Paris all her friends were older than her. But now she had got to know me, and she thought I was an easy person to like, or at least that is what she said.

We always ended with the agony aunt column. The stories amused us, even if they were not funny. We could not understand how these women could share their problems with someone they did not know. Thus, we came upon the misfortunes of one poor Geneviève.

'My husband is unfaithful to me, he never dines with me in the evening and comes home late. What shall I do?'

To which the journalist replied:

'Geneviève, your fate, alas, is that of many women. If you love your husband, continue to greet him as you do, without abandoning your calm. Reproaches would only drive him away from home, that is why I insist that you continue to be a wife in every sense of the term. Your husband will grow weary of his misconduct and will surely return to you.'

I remember this answer because of the way Madame M. reacted.

'Who does this journalist think she is? What one ought to do or not do, what one is supposed to think or not think...Is there no salvation outside their standards?! I cannot bear this sort of talk!'

She went into a terrible rage, just like that, for no particular reason. I was astonished; as a rule this column, if anything, made us laugh.

I thought back on Sophie's words, 'Since she has got to know you, Madame M. has been improving by the day,' and her husband's 'If I agreed to come and live here, it was so you would feel better.'

This woman didn't seem to be unhappy by nature; there had to be a specific cause. Why had she come to L'Escalier for refuge? Whom was she 'avoiding', as her husband put it? I sensed it would serve no purpose to ask her. Not now. Her fit of rage was merely rage, not the beginning of an explanation, and as I did not really know what to say, I had a rather silly idea. I suggested we write a letter to this 'Marie-Madeleine', as the journalist called herself, to tell her just how much we disapproved of her advice.

I had hoped in suggesting we write this letter that it might give me some clue as to what had happened to Madame M., but it didn't, she merely calmed down as quickly as she had flown off the handle. Letters to 'Mary Pigpen', however, became one of our rituals. We never sent them. Just writing them was enough to amuse us.

Madame M. might never have told me a thing if I hadn't arrived one morning at L'Escalier in a panic, in the midst of an asthma attack. 'I'm going to die, I'm going to die, I'm bleeding, look, I'm bleeding.' Madame M. immediately understood what was going on. She smiled; she too had not dared say a thing to her parents the day it happened to her. She asked Sophie to run a hot bath for me to ease the pain. I don't know how long I stayed in that bathtub looking at my belly, completely astonished by what was going on inside it. Were there many more secrets like this that life had in store?

The gong sounded for lunch, Madame M. brought me a bathrobe. When I stood up the blood began gushing down my legs again. I watched as the stain grew larger in the bathwater and I thought what a lovely painting it would make. Madame M. was also staring at the red patches that were taking some time to dissolve, and then she gave me an odd look. When I got out of the bathtub, there in front of me she took off her dress and her underwear, and she lay down in my dirty bathwater. I shall never forget, I was so embarrassed. I knew then that she would tell me everything.

*

It all began just after their wedding. Madame M. was nineteen, her husband was twenty. They had been devastated by the shocking death of their parents. They were unhappy, overwhelmed by heavy responsibilities. Her husband did not want to take over the family business. Property, land, companies: he decided to sell everything. Already all he could think of was journalism. They spent long months arranging everything and had time for nothing else. But then, as heirs, they had the inevitable reflex: what was the point of their considerable fortune if they had no one to leave it to?

In the beginning Madame M. wasn't really worried. All the women in her entourage told her she simply had to wait for nature to take its course, it was only a matter of months. And besides, their parents' death had been so sudden, one ought not to underestimate the shock.

But two years went by and nature still had not taken its course. Those couples who had got married when they did already had a child, some were even expecting their second. Madame M. was desperate. She had followed excruciating diets. She had taken medication she made up on her own, but nothing worked. Completely at a loss, she ended up inflicting torture on herself. But no matter what she tried, she did not get pregnant. Her story was horrifying. That is why she had come to settle at L'Escalier. To get away from those terrible memories.

By the time she stopped talking the water was cold, her lips were blue. Sophie was knocking on the door. Madame M. stood up, and I could not help but look at her body. Her skin was marked from her buttocks to her knees. The lesions were healing but I could still see the scars from the blows she had inflicted on herself. 'To awaken the sleeping organs', books advised 'whipping the lower back and the inner thighs until they bleed.' I could not understand how she could have subjected herself to such a thing. Her answer was chilling. 'Because that is the only advice there is for infertile women.' She had never looked at me like that. In that moment I remember thinking she no longer found me such an 'easy person to like', as she put it.

We sat down at the dinner table. Neither one of us was hungry, but we forced ourselves, so we wouldn't have to speak. It seemed to me that I understood her. In a way I missed the brother or sister I had never had as much as she missed the child she could not have. I just wanted to reassure her when I told her that some day it would work, that my parents had also waited a very long time before they had me. She didn't answer. She went on eating in silence.

After my parents, and then Madame M., I thought it was something of a coincidence, all these people around me yearning for children. And as I had never known what purpose I served in life, that day as I sat there staring at my piece of lamb I believed that my role in life would be to fight infertility. Suddenly it became absolutely clear to me. 'The room without walls', the paintings, Alberto – at last I had a way to thank her for everything she had done for me. I did not know how to tell her. The agony aunt column was there before me. I took a sheet of paper and a pencil and I wrote, reading it out loud.

'Dear Mary Pigpen, a woman I love with all my heart

cannot have a child. I don't want children. The only thing that matters to me in life is painting. So I would like to bear her child for her. That way I could, in turn, give her what she needs in life.'

Madame M. did not look up. I saw her tears flowing into her plate, she went on eating without looking at me, shaken by terrible sobs. She eventually managed to say that the young girl who was writing this letter was extremely kind, but she didn't know what she was saying, and Mary Pigpen was bound to bring her back to her senses. And then she stood up and left the dining room. We did not speak of it any more.

When, two months later, she told me she would do it, at first I did not understand. And then she murmured that we would have to be very careful so that no one would know. At the time I did not know what to say. I had made the suggestion in the heat of our conversation because everything had got muddled in my head. The idea of my recently discovered fertility. Her infertility. Her sorrow. My gratitude. Now the idea seemed a bit foolish. But I quickly reassured myself: her husband would never agree to it.

'I have managed to convince my husband: you will try just once, and if it works, it works, and if it doesn't, it doesn't. God will decide.'

She did not ask me my opinion again. She explained in minute detail how it would all come about. I would not have to do a thing, it would not take long, she promised. She had arranged everything. Her husband would be coming back within the hour and she thought it would be a good idea if we made the most of this time.

I could not believe he had agreed.

'Let's wait until tomorrow.'

That was all I managed to say. I could tell I was headed for disaster but all the courage I could muster was that of avoidance. 'Let's wait until tomorrow.' I didn't want it to happen under these conditions. Not with a man I did not know. Not for the first time.

Madame M. must have thought I was trying to wriggle out of it, but that wasn't it. I just needed some time. I would keep my promise. I couldn't go back on my word now, I had never seen her so happy. Besides, I wasn't afraid. With all her explanations it felt like I had an appointment at the doctor's. No more, no less. And that was something I was used to.

Just to be alone now. And stare at a canvas. Not to think, just not to have to think. Madame M. seemed embarrassed. When I went into the room without walls, I understood why. A bed had grown there overnight. And the mirror had vanished behind a drape that was even redder and newer than all the others. I could not stay in that room. As I walked down the driveway I passed her husband. I did not dare look at him.

But the next morning I kept our appointment. And everything went just as she had hoped. I became pregnant 'with the efficiency of a virgin'.

We left three months later. Before my clothed body could betray us. She had planned everything. We would leave the village for the duration of my pregnancy and come back after the birth. And life would go on as before. As if nothing had happened, except that at last in her arms she would be holding the infant she had so desired. How could I have believed things could be that simple?

Throughout her entire story Annie had been pacing the room, her cup of chicory between her palms. As if suddenly reminded of its existence, she put the cup down on the table and came to sit next to me again.

'You are the first person I have ever told this story to, Louis. I wrote it in a letter to my parents. But they never received it. Even though Sophie swore to me that she would post it. I shall never forgive her.'

Annie was probably expecting me to ask her questions. 'What happened?' 'Where is your child?' But as a poor jealous man I could find nothing better than to insult her.

'That kind Monsieur M. was no luckier than I was. Well, it looks like one time only is all any of us can expect from you!'

Annie's expression grew tense, she had tears in her eyes. But for once I didn't care – about her, about what had happened, about her unhappiness; all I could think of was myself and I wanted to make her pay for what I felt she still owed me, despite the years: my unrequited love.

Her wedding band was an offence to my eyes. She must not have known how to tell me she was married.

The church bell struck seven. Annie suddenly felt for the pocket of her cardigan. She said she had forgotten to leave the keys for her colleague who was supposed to close up the shop where they worked, she was sorry, she had to go back there, she couldn't afford to get herself sacked. She asked me to wait for her; she had so many things to tell me. She begged me to forgive her if she had hurt me; she hadn't meant to. She was distraught. She hurriedly put on her shoes and went out, shoelaces trailing. I listened to her footsteps as they faded away on the stairs; I had not lost my schoolboy habits.

I had been deeply troubled upon seeing her again; for almost three years I had believed that she was married or lost or even dead, and now she had reappeared in my life without warning. And she was telling me everything. I certainly had not reacted in the way she expected. But I already knew her story.

What Annie didn't know was that Sophie had indeed kept her word, and Annie's mother had indeed received her letter.

I can still see the anxious old woman dripping with rain under the awning outside my house, holding a huge umbrella. It was pouring that day. She handed me the letter. I immediately recognised Annie's handwriting. The envelope contained several pages of closely written handwriting, on both sides, as if she had been afraid she would not have enough paper. She had already been away with Madame M. for several months.

Eugénie looked distraught.

'This is so worrying, such a long letter, something must have happened!'

'For a mother, too long or too short is always a bad sign...' I replied, in what I hoped was a cheerful tone. But the length of the letter surprised me as well. Up until now Annie had never sent her anything but very laconic postcards. My expression must have changed.

'What has happened? Louis, tell me what is going on!'

The time it took for me to look up from the letter and meet her gaze it was done, I had already lied.

'Nothing. Everything is fine. Everything is fine. But I'm late, please forgive me. Go on home, I'll stop by and read it to you tonight.'

And I had rushed to my room with the letter in my hand, in order to go over it on my own. To understand how all this could have happened.

'...The next day I came as agreed and everything went just as Madame M. had hoped. I became pregnant "with the efficiency of a virgin". I will be giving birth in a few days. The child will be called Louis if it's a boy, and Louise if it's a girl. I am so afraid, afraid of dying and never seeing you again. I love you. I hope you can forgive me.'

These were, more or less, the only words Annie had written to her parents that she had not repeated to me in her account.

I copied out these few pages into an exercise book, to have a record of them, then I sat under the awning and watched as they melted in the rain. I had decided not to read them to Eugénie: it would be too cruel, she was too fragile. Annie pregnant with another woman's baby: she could not bear it. Even I could not understand how it was possible – how could she have allowed that man to make her pregnant?

As I watched the raindrops softening the paper I tried to find comfort in the thought that one often regrets confiding in others out of fear, and Annie would be relieved to know what I had done. And besides, I was not destroying the truth, merely deferring it. If by the time she got back from her journey she still wanted her mother to know what had happened, then she would tell her. But at that moment I sincerely thought I was acting for the best as far as everyone was concerned.

The letter was illegible. The ink had spread in huge blots. I apologised ten times over to Eugénie, I had left the letter on my desk, I hadn't noticed that the window was open, I was so sorry.

So I had to make up another story – the war had just begun, the confusion on the front, all sorts of things which – and this did surprise me – Annie had not mentioned at all in her letter. But I reckoned that with everything she was going through she must have her mind on other things, and then again perhaps in the South of France the tension was less noticeable than here.

Eugénie nevertheless found my version rather short in comparison to the length of the letter. I replied that things always seemed shorter when spoken than when they were written. I was ashamed to be taking advantage of her weakness, but I knew she would not say anything. I was right: she nodded her head humbly, without daring to ask anything else. She took my fabricated rule for a golden one, and merely remarked happily that her little girl had regained something of her talkativeness.

I had never asked Eugénie why she had picked me to read her daughter's letters to her. Had she sensed I was a young admirer who would be easy to corner? Did she hope I would read them out loud without paying attention? Or that I would talk to her about them, thus relating the precious contents?

'I don't know how to read.'

She could not have asked me the time of day in a more offhand manner, but bent over on the stool in the passage she eventually murmured that it was a real torment for her. No matter how many hours she spent staring at Annie's letters, she couldn't understand a thing. At night she would go to bed hoping for a miracle, but in the morning nothing had changed. She felt utterly stupid because of a pile of letters. She had never told anyone. Neither her husband. Nor Annie. She had always managed to keep them from finding out.

Eugénie was crying, blowing her nose fitfully. Even the day Annie had come home sobbing because Mademoiselle E. had told her that any mother who loves her children reads them stories – even that day, she had managed to find a way round it.

'I don't read you stories…that's true…but that has nothing to do with love…Love is…it's more mysterious than that…Where love is concerned, my darling, you mustn't ask, mustn't beg. Don't ever try to make people love you the way you want them to love you, that's not it, that's not true love. You have to let people love you their own way, and my way, it isn't about reading you stories, but it might be about sewing you all the dresses I can, and all the coats, skirts and scarves that you love so much. Aren't we happy like that? You don't want another maman, do you? Tell me, Annie, you don't want another maman?'

After that day Annie had never reproached her again. Eugénie thought that was one worry she'd got rid of for good. Even when Annie had told them she wanted to go away with Madame M. for a few months, Eugénie wasn't particularly worried. No matter how often her husband told her he wanted nothing to do with a daughter who would abandon them for some *bourgeoise*, Eugénie knew that he would read her letters, and that he would write to her. He loved Annie too deeply to carry out any of his threats. But when the first card arrived, Eugénie was trapped; her husband had just been arrested, and she had no one to turn to. It had taken several cards before she got up the nerve to confess to me that she didn't know how to read. Had she found her resolve by telling herself again and again that I was as worthy of her trust as the hundreds of metres of fabric that she had bought from my mother?

And it would seem she was right. I never betrayed her secret.

I have always thought that secrets must die with those who have harboured them. You must surely be thinking that I am betraying my own convictions since I am sharing them with you, but to you, I must tell everything.

'I have always thought that secrets must die with those who have harboured them. You must surely be thinking that I am betraying my own convictions since I am sharing them with you, but to you, I must tell everything.'

I was overcome by an unpleasant feeling. The author of these letters really was writing to someone. In a burst of anger that surprised me I tossed the sheets of paper across the room.

I stood livid before the mirror. I saw myself closing my eyes and heard myself say, 'Don't worry, come on, it's all just fiction.' But once I had calmed down, I realised that I was afraid.

Why had I tried to change the course of events? I was pacing back and forth in Annie's room, I felt terribly guilty. It was all my fault. Why hadn't I read the letter to Eugénie? But in that room that was too small for my remorse I had not been able to confess as much to Annie. I had only just found her, I could not bear the idea of losing her again, or of making her angry with me. Three years without seeing her.

Even her absence for a few hours over the business with the keys made me feel sick.

And besides, I would have been forced to betray her mother's secret; Annie would surely ask me why I was the one reading her letters.

I didn't know what to do with myself. I was desperate for Annie to come back.

I remember I washed the tray and our cups, looked at the handful of books on the shelf, and straightened the crucifix over her bed. I leafed distractedly through the calendar to see what the coming days had in store. 'Thunder in October, plentiful grape harvest': so went the saying for that 4 October 1943.

All that fiddling with an aim to avoid doing what, in the end, I did anyway: open her dresser. Men's clothing, belonging to her husband. And her own. Three dresses, two cardigans that were too light for the season, stockings rolled up in a ball and ugly underwear. I needed so badly to imbibe her scent that I hunted for her dirty laundry. Obscene. But because in the beginning my love for Annie had been chaste, I had no difficulty in loving her lustfully, my back against the door so I would not be caught out. Her full breasts hanging down: I had been obsessed by that image ever since the day when she had asked me to help her move a bench to prepare the theatre performance. She had leaned forward first, and her bodice had opened. She hadn't noticed a thing, not the movement of the cloth, or the movement of my eyes. For a long time I dreamed of her breasts at that angle, hanging down, round and hanging, her breasts where I would have liked to…I came.

'"Let's wait until tomorrow." I didn't want it to happen under these conditions. Not with a man I did not know. Not for the first time.'

I suddenly understood what Annie had been referring to in her story, and I choked on the memory of it.

I had indeed always been the first.

For several months already the fact that she was seeing Madame M. had distanced Annie from me. I was hardly expecting her to come by the house for me. She dragged me to the lake, bypassing the towpath; I had the impression she wanted to tell me something. After a while she stopped.

'Come on, in you go.'

I stayed on the shore, motionless, speechless. 'In you go...' I had already heard those words somewhere. Another woman, in another place. That place had been as damp as could be; there was a smell of mildew, which was hardly surprising, all the windows were boarded up and the door to that 'house' was the one that was opened and closed again faster than any door in town. Violette came up to me, never taking her eyes from me.

'Come on, in you go...'

In spite of my fear I smiled. Once we were in, the rooms were actually downstairs. But you don't chicken out after a password like that one...Violette went down and I followed her, feeling that, with this virile endeavour, I was going one step further in my story with Annie. There are not many women who enjoy being taken by a man for whom it's the first time.

'Come on, in you go...'

This time, the expression was in keeping with the layout of the place. Once I had regained my self-control I grabbed hold of the rope to pull the boat closer to the bank.

Annie climbed into the boat and I followed.

The boat was wider than it was deep. We lay on our backs to avoid being seen. Annie seemed preoccupied. I had the impression she wanted to tell me something, but she didn't say anything. The sky must often serve as an excuse for awkward lovers, but we were not so lucky; it was too early for stars. And with my eyes riveted on the empty sky I felt lost. This time I was all alone. There was no Violette to guide me. I searched my memories in vain, I could not recall how it had started with her. I did not know which gesture, which caress to choose. Violette had undressed herself, displaying no particular fervour, no particular boldness, simply her slow, migraine-sufferer gestures, and the detachment that comes with habit. Clumsily I unbuttoned Annie's shirt, one tiny fastener after the other. She was wearing sensible spring clothes, for that notorious month of 'April showers'. Violette had the type of skin of women who do not look after their bodies, knowing it will be put to good use no matter what. Annie's skin was smooth and soft. If she had kept her eyes open – like Violette – she would have seen that I was looking at her ample breasts against her slender chest. No, she wouldn't have, because if her eyes had been open I would not have dared to look at her breasts. Her fists were clenched, too. Violette and I had been naked. Annie and I kept as many clothes on as possible. Violette had made me stroke her with my hand. Beneath my fingers I had discovered those rough patches, when in fact I had always thought it would be smooth. 'It's good when it's wet like that,' she said quietly, like a comment, a lesson. She had let go of my hand and I felt hers come gently to rest on my sex, where my entire body was concentrated, and then her body had replaced her hand. It's good when it's wet like that, I tried to reassure myself, my hand between Annie's thighs.

Nothing in Violette's body had distracted my attention. Everything in Annie's troubled me. Violette's face had suddenly relaxed, whereas Annie's grew tense. I could not stand it, still less the sight of her body arching, lifting her chest in an upward movement that overwhelmed me.

Everything had gone well with Violette. But with Annie, badly.

She quickly pulled down her skirt. I quickly pulled up my trousers. Once we were dressed, we both felt better. Above all to be together. I was afraid that Annie might leave right away, but she didn't, we went on lying there facing the stars that had still not come out. Again I had the impression that Annie had something to tell me, but she said nothing.

To this day, I am still angry with myself for not having found the necessary courage. I had found the courage to make love to her, badly, but not to get her to speak. I could have stopped her from going to her appointment with Monsieur M. and then none of this would ever have happened.

I was overwhelmed with emotion. I had indeed always been the first. Annie had not lied. Or at least, not about that.

Because if she had fallen pregnant from Monsieur M. 'with the efficiency of a virgin', as she liked to say, she should have left three months later: April…May…June. So, in July.

But she had left the day after Christmas, and that was something I remembered clearly. I had gone to her house to give her a little present, which in rage I threw against a tree on my way back home. She had just left with Madame M.

July…August…September…October…November… December…

So there were five months missing from Annie's story; that was a lot.

If the door to her bedroom had not suddenly banged against my back, I might have guessed what had happened during that lapse of time she had conjured away.

I quickly got to my feet, tossing the underwear beneath the dresser to get rid of it. If this was her husband coming home, I would have to restrain myself from smashing him in the face. Annie fell into my arms so eagerly that I got a lump in my throat: she had honestly been afraid I would no longer be there when she got back. She had been quick. She took a strange statue out of her bag, a long-legged woman seated on a sort of chair, her hands open wide around the empty space as if she were holding an invisible object in front of her belly, and that was the name of the statue, 'the Invisible Object'. It was a gift from Alberto that she had brought back from the shop to show me. She put it on the table but, rather than sitting down, she suggested that we go out.

This was the day that she normally went to the municipal baths; did I mind going there with her?

I found it somewhat strange, how eager she was suddenly to have a wash, but I did not dwell upon it. I supposed she was in a hurry because of the curfew. I hoped the fresh air would help me recover my wits, but Annie did not give me any respite. No sooner were we in the street than she continued her story where she had left off in order to go and drop off the keys. Without making any mention, naturally, of the mysterious months that had vanished. It would be years before I learned anything more about them.

Madame M. had planned everything. For the duration of my pregnancy we would move to their home in Paris, where they used to live before they came to L'Escalier. Above all we must say nothing to my parents; they would not understand why I didn't go to see them from time to time. As far as anyone knew we had gone a long way away, in the south. To Collioure, where the climate was gentler. We had to find a pretext for our departure. And if war did break out, even though it did not seem to be heading that way, at least we would be in a safe place. Madame M. had an explanation for everything.

I felt uncomfortable lying to my parents. She offered to tell them for me. It wouldn't cost her anything and she had planned to come to the house in any case, to meet them and reassure them. My father didn't say a word. He sat there ramrod straight in his armchair. Maman didn't even try to ease the tension. She was too sad to pretend otherwise. But Madame M. was not one to get flustered. She was a very good liar. That should have alerted me. My father asked me if I really wanted to go there with that woman for the duration of her pregnancy. I said I did. So, without even getting to his feet he ordered Madame M. to leave his house immediately.

After that things became unbearable. My father accused me of abandoning them for a *bourgeoise* who was pregnant from a capitalist. Filthy rich parasites. That was his new refrain. Whenever I made the mistake of looking at him he would order me to stop judging him. The moment I didn't help myself to seconds it was 'mademoiselle has become a picky eater ever since she started sharing her lunches with the duchess'. One evening he went too far and I lost my temper. It was time he stopped exaggerating, I was not 'abandoning' them, they had managed to live forty years without me, they would survive five short months, and besides, we would write to each other, it wasn't the end of the world…

I am sorry that I spoke to them like that. I should never have left them, but how was I to know? I thought about everything I was about to discover in Paris. If it had been up to me alone, we would have left even earlier. But I felt so sorry for Maman. I didn't manage to reassure her. Her maternal intuition, I suppose. The final weeks were tricky. I fled from her measuring tape like the plague. She kept telling me what it was like when her breasts had started to grow; she'd got it into her head that this was why I wouldn't let her take my measurements. 'I'm the one who made you, after all!' she said, again and again. She was so kind, Maman. Yet I had to keep pushing her away. In fact, I couldn't stop thinking of a story that you had told me, about

Rodin. Do you remember? About a sitting where he discovered that one of his models was pregnant before the girl herself even knew. Well, I was sure the same thing would happen with Maman. Even with her eyes closed she could tell. She knew my body too well: as she said, she was the one who had made me. Nor could I buy new clothes to camouflage my belly – she would have really taken it as an insult.

Luckily my seams held up until Christmas. My last Christmas with my parents. I was three months pregnant. Papa gave me an easel he had made himself, bigger than the other one because I had grown. Well, no, he didn't exactly give it to me. He was too proud for that. I found it under the Christmas tree. Covered in a lovely sea-green woollen cape. 'I knitted it myself, thinking of what it feels like to hold you in my arms.' I let Maman hold me tight, even though I usually wouldn't let her near me any more. Papa didn't even want a thank-you kiss for the easel. I cried. But not in his presence, anything but that.

The next day was the big departure. I left with Madame M. at night. No one must see me arrive at their house. She had prepared everything. I would take Sophie's room under the eaves. That way I could open the window without any risk, as there were no facing windows. On the way she explained that no one must know I was there. When she had visitors I would stay in my room. When she went out as well. Because, in spite of the curtains, passers-by or neighbours would be able to see whether someone was in a room. And if they had just run into her in the street or elsewhere, they would wonder who was in the house. I complied with these arrangements without protesting. I divided my time between Sophie's room and the bathroom next door, where there was no window either. When Madame M. was there and I wanted to stretch my legs, she would come up to my room. The rest of the time we spent there together. In that respect it was not that different from L'Escalier. I painted. She read. Except that it was a bit cramped.

And to think I had believed I'd be discovering Paris!

In those days the news from the front was still good. The war no longer took up the headlines. Maybe just one or two columns. Just enough to show all the soldiers languishing on the Maginot line that they had not been forgotten. Ever since we read that they were planting roses there to boost the troops' morale we lost any fear of a full-scale war. Mobilisation wasn't war, that's what you read everywhere. It was nothing but a 'Phoney War'. We amused ourselves trying to guess the words that had been blacked out in the papers. We spent some time on it. There were so many blanks that certain articles were illegible.

'Twelve people had to be hospitalised in Paris after they slipped on a patch of [...] covering the pavement.'

'Ice!'

'Well done!'

Even weather forecasts were forbidden: they might be useful to the enemy.

Madame M.'s unbridled cheerfulness was completely new to me. She went out a great deal, but did not neglect me for all that. She told me how she spent her time – the races at Longchamp, the charity sales for the soldiers...She told me about people. She gave me fashionable clothing with names and colours inspired by the events. A 'tank' coat. An 'extended leave' nightgown. They weren't really useful to me, given 'the present state of affairs', meaning my huge belly, but I would give them to my mother when we went back to the village, and she'd be able to use them as models to make clothing for the women there. They'd snatch them up like hotcakes. I thought Madame M. was being very considerate.

I tried to capture the new tones with my palette. 'Maginot' blue. 'Aeroplane' grey. A 'French soil' beige. I mixed my paints to drive away my darker thoughts. I no longer knew what to paint. I was thinking too much, so I copied things. That was better than nothing.

She knew it was hard for me to be shut away in that house. She had pinned a map of Paris to the wall in my room so that I would not feel so far away from everything. Before she left the house she would show me where she was going. I spent hours repeating the names of streets. I studied the different arrondissements, while my belly grew ever rounder. She also brought me photographs and postcards from all sorts of places. The Eiffel Tower, the Place de la Concorde, the Arc de Triomphe. The Louvre. She promised me we would visit all these places together after the birth. She made so many plans for the future, 'for afterwards', as she put it. I ought to have seen through her words, the way I could fill in the censored blanks. But not for one instant did I suspect what she had in store for me. She was really very kind to me.

She brought me a kitten so I wouldn't feel so lonely when she wasn't there. All grey, with a reddish patch on the top of its head. I called it Alto, in honour of Alberto. I missed his lessons. She had told him I was back in the village. And that we would start up our lessons again when she went back to L'Escalier, after the birth. Alberto lived in Paris, she couldn't tell him I was here, he wouldn't have understood why I didn't just go to his studio. It all seemed very complicated to me. Not to her. She wiggled her way out of any potential trap with ease.

She had also moved the wireless up to my room, to keep me company. I listened to it a lot, mostly music. I turned up the volume for the baby. I told myself we were alike, the two of us: we could only hear faceless voices.

I called it *the baby*. She called it *my baby*. I didn't say anything. There were plenty of other things I didn't say to her. To stop putting her hands on my belly all the time. To stop giving me advice for her baby, to the effect that I had to eat properly for her baby. Sleep properly for her baby. Keep the bedroom window open, the smell of paint was not good for her baby. What was good or not good for her baby – that was all that interested her.

We had the same figure. The towels she strapped around her middle grew thicker and thicker as my own belly grew. She never removed them. Even at home. She copied all my gestures. I hated it. You would have thought she was really pregnant. In any case, everyone in her entourage believed it.

She didn't want to miss a thing about this pregnancy that she considered to be *her* pregnancy. She shouldn't have asked me so many questions. She was constantly asking me whether I felt them, those little champagne bubbles. Her friends who were already mothers always asked her that question and she didn't know what to reply. I couldn't tell what sensation they were talking about. Perhaps my pregnancy wasn't normal. The idea that I wasn't pregnant at all had even crossed my mind, perhaps I was just a little girl again, a little girl whose menses had fled when they understood what I planned to do with them. When this thought occurred to me I was relieved. It meant that this farce would soon come to an end. That I would regain my freedom. Go home. See my parents again. See you again. And then one evening, buried under my eiderdown, I felt it. There, down at the very bottom of my belly. Much lower down than I expected. A first time. Then again. And then yet again. But it wasn't like champagne bubbles. It was like the fluttering of tiny fish. I couldn't say it was like champagne bubbles, I had never drunk champagne. But I had seen little fish, on the surface of the lake in the rain.

As the weeks went by this fluttering turned into quivering. Very faint to begin with. Then more and more obvious. Until before long my belly was contorted by the blows. From a foot. From a hand. From an elbow. My baby was moving about in a space that was too small for it. Just like I was.

The only events I was entitled to be part of were those taking place in my womb. How could I not be alert to them, and describe them in detail? Grow attached to them? Before my belly began to grow, I was still honest. It was afterwards that things started getting out of control. The more I answered Madame M.'s questions, the further I retreated from my promise. But perhaps I would have distanced myself no matter what. Perhaps this idea of wanting to bear a child for someone else was only an illusion right from the start. I don't know. And yet others have done it.

At night I could not sleep. My stomach was burning. To fight boredom I would perform memory exercises. I would wander around the house, and I had to remember where each object was located in one room in order to have the right to move on to the next room. I told myself it was a good exercise for copying, in painting. But above all it allowed me to speak to the baby without speaking about us. I taught it about the world of things. 'You see, this is a book, that's a vase, I don't know what that is, let's call it "the blue object", that's just bad taste, that's a drawer, this is ammunition, this is a little pistol.'

I retraced my parents' features, especially my mother's. I could not help but say to the baby, 'You see, those are your grandparents.' They were the only human beings I spoke to the baby about.

I wondered what its face would be like. Its eyes. Hair. Body. I hoped it would look like me in every respect. That it would come out of me looking so much like me that she could never bring herself to take it from me, because she would be so convinced that when people saw them together they would say, 'That's your friend Annie, she's shrunk.'

I had suggested names to her, and she went along with them. It didn't matter to her. She wanted a child, not a name. I didn't like the tone of her reply. I had to refrain from answering back that it wasn't a child she wanted, but *my* child. I would have liked to go back on my word, but I knew that was impossible, she would never agree to it. I had no qualms any more about asking her to buy me supplies; now we were equal. I wished she would stop putting up with all my requests and just throw me out. I wanted to run away. Even if it meant giving birth in the street. And then? Shame. Unwed mother. Less than nothing. I had heard too many stories like that not to know. If my parents had been younger, we could have said it was their child. I wouldn't be the first to become the sister of my own child. 'Annie must be pleased not to be an only child any more,' people would say, 'she's been complaining about it for so long.'

But it was not possible, no one would believe it. And the greatest misfortune of all was that deep down I was convinced my child would have a greater chance at happiness in Madame M.'s world than in mine. Isn't that why I had gone away with her? With a sinking heart I counted the days until the birth. And it was as if she could read my thoughts. One evening she came to reassure me. I could see the child whenever I saw fit, we could stay together if I liked, at least until her husband came back from the war, and even afterwards, he would surely agree, it was really up to me if she kept me on as a wet-nurse, and later, when the child was old enough, we'd see, we would try to explain things. She didn't believe a damned word she was saying. But I did. I could no longer bear the idea of losing my child. I needed to believe her. I felt so alone.

All through those long months in Paris I didn't receive a single letter from my parents. I thought that my father must be keeping his word. 'You want to see what it's like to go far away, well then you will see, don't count on us to write to you.' That's what he said just after he gave me the easel. I knew he had a temper, but for once I thought this was being too spiteful. At the same time, since I had never made him this angry before, because of this trip, I figured I was just getting acquainted with the extreme side of his temperament. And I felt sorry for Maman. She must have spent all her time trying to defend me. I missed her so much. I would have liked to share these moments with her, to find out what she had felt when I was in her womb.

'Your parents are fine.' That was what Madame M. always passed on. Beaming. 'Your parents are fine.' Filthy liar.

Jacques, Monsieur M.'s handyman, had stayed behind at L'Escalier. 'To look after the place until we get back,' she said. Because of his gammy leg, he had not been called up. He was the one who came up to Paris once a week with news of my parents, but I never saw him, I only heard his voice. She didn't want him to find out about me, either. The only one who knew, apart from the two of us, was Sophie. Madame M. gave my letters to Jacques and he took them to my parents, a temporary postman. Because at least I wrote to them. Not a lot. But often. It was hard to find things to write about. Even talking about the weather would be complicated. I had to write as if I was in Collioure. And above all as if I was not pregnant.

My parents believed that my letters were part of a package that Madame M. sent to Jacques. All so that a postmark would not betray us. She left nothing up to chance. Before our departure she had even managed to get hold of twenty or more postcards of Collioure. Some of them were the same: she thought that would be even more credible, it's always like that, lots of people send the same card twice from a place without realising.

She read my letters before she gave them to Jacques, I'm sure. She would never have run the risk that I might write something that would betray us. She didn't tell me, but I knew. I thought of her as my chief censor. Fair enough, there were also things I didn't tell her.

She often asked to look at my belly. She would stare at it until the little bump appeared and moved across it. I could see how troubled she was to see this. She would look at me with the eyes of the dispossessed. I didn't try to convince her otherwise. We all have our cross to bear. Hers was what she was living through now. Mine lay ahead of me. When the baby would be in her arms.

And I lied to her. As the weeks passed, I lied more and more often in response to her invasive questioning. When she asked me if I felt something when the child kicked, I said no, I didn't feel a thing. Which was completely untrue. But she believed me. She had no other way of knowing. And I enjoyed imagining her at her dinners on the town, repeating my words, 'No, I didn't feel a thing.' And I was delighted at the thought of the incredulous looks the other women would give her.

The only thing I felt like painting was my own body. But I knew that she wouldn't be able to stand the sight of canvases of my pregnancy invading the room, so I had to make do with moments when she wasn't there. The moment a sketch was finished, I had to hurry to cover it with something else, something flat. Frequently a blue sky. She must have thought I was painting a lot of skies. But as that was all I could see of the outside world, through the window, she must not have found it very surprising.

This sinister comedy lasted one hundred and seventy-four days. One hundred and seventy-four days of prison, less sixteen days.

She woke me up in the middle of the night. She had a surprise for me. The car was waiting for us outside the house. Scarcely an hour later we pulled up outside a mill. I thought this was just a stopping-off place; it was our destination. She wanted me to get some fresh air. It wasn't luxurious, but it would be good for her baby. There was a kitchen. A very long main room. A sort of alcove for washing. And a bedroom. The rooms in the basement were uninhabitable. Full of dust and milling equipment. I was astonished we had come to this place. It was neither comfortable nor clean. But I could go out. I felt alive again. I spent my time out of doors. It was the end of March, nature was awakening. I had brought my sketchbook and charcoal with me. I found some inspiration again. I was the only one who made the most of the place. Along with Alto, who followed me everywhere. As for Madame M., she never left the mill. She spent her days sprawled in a chair by the window doing crossword puzzles. She stayed there, tense, startled by the slightest noise. I could see she was afraid we might be found out. I could also see she was afraid I might run away. I would have liked to. But I was seven months pregnant. And I had already felt a few contractions. It would have been too risky to follow the stream until I found someone to help me. Not to mention the fact that now I knew what she was like. If we were there, it was because there was no one within a radius of at least ten kilometres.

We had never been so far apart. And yet we slept in the same bed. There was only one bed. Sophie slept on a mat in the kitchen. Madame M. came to bed once I was asleep, and she got up at dawn. We never touched. Each of us on either side of our 'Maginot line'. I didn't sleep well. I would look at this odd scene: two pregnant women lying in the same bed. Our huge bellies distorting the blankets. A camel was sleeping in this room. I was thinking on behalf of the child in my belly: there's the camel that has two humps and there's the dromedary with only one…I would have to be able to answer all my child's questions.

Madame M. wasn't sleeping well either. She was agitated and talked in her sleep. I felt like smothering her with her belly, tearing off all those deceiving towels and stuffing them in her mouth until she died. And she was sweating. In the morning her spot in the bed was soaked. We couldn't wash the sheets and that acrid smell filled the room. I felt like telling her that her stench wasn't good for the baby. One day I joked about it with Sophie. The following night I was awoken by the contact of a leg against mine. The two-humped camel had changed into a dromedary. I lifted the sheet, cautiously, and was astonished to see she had removed her belly. In fact she hadn't removed a thing, it was Sophie who had taken her place next to me. The next morning Madame M. told me that if she was talking in her sleep it must be keeping me awake and that wasn't good for her baby.

We stayed there for sixteen days and then we went back to Paris. I gave birth less than two months later.

She came into my room and handed me a doll.

'Look what I just bought.'

'She's lovely.'

'More than that. Press the button behind her neck.'

'Maman! Maman!'

On hearing the doll's words I felt a violent contraction.

Any pregnant woman would be disturbed by these letters, at least that's how I rationalised my reaction.

I had distanced myself from the correspondence and was convinced it was a novel, or probably a memoir. But there was still no sign of the author.

I missed my mother a great deal, too; I too would have liked to know what she felt when I was in her womb; I too felt alone.

I have often noticed that with each birth comes a death. As if there were a quota for the number of souls on earth. I did not have to wait long for this terrible conjuring trick to become a reality. My own mother died four days after I informed her that I was pregnant. Losing your mother a few days after becoming a mother yourself makes you feel terribly isolated.

I still cannot grasp the fact that my child will never know her.

Why the fuck did she have to drive so fast on that country road?

After I folded up the letter I almost called Nicolas. Maybe running away from him was not such a good solution after all, any more than hiding my pregnancy from him. At least I could give him the option of saying no. I knew he didn't want anything to do with it, but at least I could let him tell me in his own words. So that I'd get over him, too.

My feelings for him will surely not survive hearing him begging me on his knees to get an abortion, telling me again and again that we haven't known each other long enough, that later, maybe, but just now it's too soon.

I used to think abortion was a good thing: progress, a woman's free will...Now I find myself struggling in a trap which, like every trap, once smelled sweetly, in this case of freedom. Progress for women, my arse! If I keep the child, I'm guilty vis-à-vis Nicolas, who doesn't want it. If I get rid of it, I am guilty vis-à-vis the baby. Abortion may claim to rescue women from the slavery of motherhood, but it imposes another form of slavery: guilt. More than ever, it is on our own that we handle or mishandle motherhood.

I would have preferred not to have to choose. Shit, if I cannot, at the age of thirty-five, take responsibility for the outcome of a night's fucking that no one forced upon me, then what can I take responsibility for? If we are no longer responsible for the lives we bring into the world, where the hell are we headed? What *can* we feel responsible for?

That was how I announced my pregnancy to my mother. She sat down with the shock. I hadn't even thought of telling her to sit down, I thought they only did that sort of thing in bad advertisements. We had never talked about it, and she had always thought I didn't want children. She was dumbstruck.

Of course I've always wanted children, I just hadn't found the right guy, and in this case I thought I'd found him but I got pregnant before I knew whether he'd go along with it, and the night I went to tell him he pulled the rug from under my feet by informing me that his brother had just had a baby and that he wouldn't like to be in his shoes, he didn't feel ready at all, not at all.

Obviously after that I wasn't able to tell him, but I've thought it over carefully, and I'm going to keep this baby, no matter what he thinks. I don't care, I'm thirty-five, nature isn't going to wait.

Maman told me she understood. I told her she'd be a wonderful grandmother. She replied, 'I'm sure'. And then she added that having a child was a good thing, but it was even better to have it with someone.

When I thought back on the strangely solemn way Maman had said those words, I promised myself I'd pick up the phone the next time Nicolas tried to get in touch with me. I had to speak to him.

The birth was terrible. I had the worst asthma attack of my entire life. It was Sophie who looked after me. She kept on saying, 'Poor Annie, poor Annie'. At one point she felt she would not be able to manage on her own and she asked Madame M. to fetch the doctor. I saw clearly that she was hesitating to fetch him. 'She's taking her time coming back. Surely she wouldn't do that, would she?' Sophie was furious. I had never seen her get angry with Madame M.

And then, I don't know what happened, I was in so much pain that I passed out. All I know is that when Madame M. came back she was alone. She never went to fetch the doctor. Can you imagine? She would rather we died, the baby and I, than let her secret become known. She was at the church, or so she said, praying for us. Thanks a lot!

I had lost a great deal of blood. Sophie was distraught; she stayed by my side for hours, even after Louise was born. It wasn't for her employer's sake that she was concerned about my life, it was for my own sake, as simple as that. She told me, she would never forgive herself if something happened to me.

I was afraid. I had come to realise just how far Madame M. was prepared to go. If she was capable of letting me die, she was capable of killing me, particularly now that Louise was born. Even today I suspect that if Sophie had not been with us, she would have. Sophie told me I was mad to think like that, that her employer would never go that far. But I had seen in her eyes that she was no longer altogether sure. And before she left my room, under cover of plumping the pillows under my head, she whispered that she would make sure Madame M. went nowhere near my food.

Louise was born on 16 May 1940.

A few days before the birth I wrote a letter to my parents telling them everything, the letter I mentioned to you a while ago. But I hadn't found a way to get it to them. That was when I thought of asking Sophie. My parents had to read that letter, my mind wouldn't be at rest until they did. If something happened to me, they had to know they had a granddaughter. I didn't want her to send it through Jacques, I didn't trust him. I had never liked the way he looked at me. Sophie told me I was wrong to think that way about him, that he was a good sort, but if I would rather she posted the letter, she would post it. She swore to me she would. She seemed sincere. I thought I could trust her. I told myself she would agree to do it because she was afraid of being accessory to a tragedy. A murder, even. But she must have changed her mind when she stood there by the letter box; she couldn't do this to her employers, they had always been good to her – she was Jewish and they had even managed to get her naturalised. So she didn't post it. And she never told me. That must be what happened.

But I made her pay for it. She shouldn't have lied to me.

It took me a while to recover from the birth. I was very weak. Madame M. never left our room. As in the beginning, we were always in the same room, but I didn't paint any more and she didn't read. We looked at Louise. We had become silent enemies. When I was breastfeeding, I could feel her jealous gaze upon me, but at least she could not steal those moments from me. For the rest, I had no choice. No choice but to let her change the baby. Take her in her arms. Rock her. Whisper into her ear. Call her 'my baby'. She took her out for walks while I stayed in bed; I couldn't get up.

I knew I wanted to go away with Louise, to go home, I no longer felt any guilt whatsoever. This was my child. But I couldn't tell Madame M. that we'd made a mistake, that you cannot separate a child from its mother, that it is against the laws of nature. She wouldn't have listened to me. She was beyond that. I had to go on pretending, had to keep on coping. Staying submissive, particularly as she must not suspect what I intended to do. I just needed long enough to regain my strength. I would find a way, sooner or later, to run away with Louise.

But I waited too long.

I was only just beginning to be able to walk again without getting tired. She came into my room one morning, as usual, at feeding time. Louise was nearly a month old. She took her from my arms and went out. I followed her. The door to her room was locked. Louise was crying. I knew how she cried and this was not her usual crying. I knocked. No answer. Only Louise, crying louder and louder. I began to be afraid. I called out to Sophie, to get her to do something. I searched every room for her and that was when I went into the bathroom.

It was horrible. My cat Alto was floating in the bath, dead. Madame M. had killed him. Drowned, strangled, I don't know, the water was full of blood. I ran back to her bedroom. I begged her to open the door. Louise had stopped crying. I was so terrified she might have hurt her. I wanted to go for help, but the front door was also locked.

Suddenly I heard her voice behind me. 'Go away! You have no business here any more.' She was at the top of the stairs. She was blocking my way. I asked her what she had done with my baby. She answered that she hadn't done anything to my baby because I had no baby. She was sincerely sorry for me, she hoped that some day I might have a child of my own, but in the meanwhile she was asking me to stop harassing her. She said I was raving mad and had only one thing in mind, to kidnap her child. It would be better if I left, now. For everyone's sake. She said 'everyone' in such a determined tone of voice that it was as if there were puppet's strings tugging me and I left the house in spite of myself.

I had finally grasped that this woman would rather kill Louise than lose her. I started down the street. I had to get away from the house. Away from her gaze, in case she was looking out the window. Do not provoke her. Let her calm down. I went round the corner and sat on a bench to regain my senses.

But right there in front of me I saw soldiers with black boots and green gloves. This couldn't be, they couldn't be here. I followed them and found myself on the Champs-Elysées. It was as if I could not awaken from my nightmare. Everywhere there were tanks, lorries, armoured cars belonging to the Wehrmacht. They were setting up machine guns at every crossroads. Cavalrymen and foot soldiers spilling onto every street. This couldn't be them: the newspapers had described the soldiers as puny, sickly, poorly dressed. These soldiers were strapping lads – proud, handsome, kitted out with gleaming weapons and new leather. But I recognised their metallic language, with its sharp accentuation. The Germans had arrived. Paris was occupied. And she hadn't told me. I looked at them, wide-eyed. Absurd tourists: they were taking photographs. I thought they were going to arrest me. But they weren't even looking at me. I was the only one with my head up who was not in uniform. The rare passers-by I encountered hurried on their way, staring at the ground. I don't know how I managed not to collapse. I wanted so badly just to turn round and go and fetch Louise.

I walked down the avenue. I turned onto the Pont de la Concorde. I crossed the Seine. Before me, a dozen German soldiers had climbed up onto the roof of the Palais-Bourbon. They had unfurled an immense banner, *Deutschland siegt an allen Fronten*. I didn't understand what it meant, but in any case, I didn't like the sound of it. I took the Boulevard Saint-Germain. They were already nailing up all their signs in German, to show which way to go. Soldiers, like monkeys, were hanging their Nazi flags. Black, white, red, swastikas were fluttering everywhere. Some of them were immense, hanging from a roof and reaching down to the ground. I could no longer see the façades. Paris, the city without walls. The swastika made me think of a labyrinth, where every way out was blocked off, but I went on walking. I saw people in their apartments, their noses against the windows, terrified. I made my way through the city like a sickly robot. Boulevard Raspail. French kepis and helmets were attached like sinister trophies to the bonnets of German cars. I came upon some prisoners but I did not dare look at them. I was afraid I might recognise someone. The sun was scorching. I would have liked to stop and take a deep breath, but I hardly dared breathe at all. I sat down frequently to regain my strength. The aeroplanes made me dizzy. Motorcars drove by with loudhailers shouting that anyone found in the street after eight p.m. would be executed. Rue des Plantes. Suddenly there were no more road signs, no more flags, no more Germans hurrying everywhere, just emptiness, silence in the deserted streets, closed shutters. If they had not yet had time to mark their territory, they were here all the same. Filthy dogs. Rue de la Sablière. 3. 14. 32. 46. I don't know how I managed to find Alberto's studio. 46, rue Hippolyte-Maindron. Perhaps the puppet strings, once again. One day, she had shown me on the map where he lived. I had gone that way several times, in my imagination, and now I went down the little passageway into the tiny courtyard. I wanted to tell Alberto everything. I thought he of all people would believe me, and that he would help me to get Louise back. He knew Madame M. well; he would make her see reason. But he wasn't there.

I don't know how long I waited there, lying on his doorstep. Two days. Three days. He woke me up, shaking me. He rushed into his studio like a madman and fell to the ground, scratching at the dirt. He had buried his statues. The ones he cared for the most. They were still there. He was so relieved, he had seen so many houses that had been ransacked. He was sure it was thanks to me. He didn't ask me what I was doing there. It was as if it were normal. As if I had come to lie down outside his door to keep watch over his treasures. Like a good dog. He was too upset by what he had just experienced to ask me any questions.

They had left Paris at the last minute. When it became too dangerous to stay. When there was no longer any doubt that the Germans were about to enter the city. He had taken his bicycle and left with Diego, his brother. They wanted to reach Bordeaux and find a ship for America. But it was chaos on the roads. Thousands and thousands of people were fleeing. Stukas were flying overhead. They made it to Etampes just after an attack. All the buildings were rubble. People were screaming. There were bits of bodies everywhere and an entire coach-load of children burned to death. They didn't stop. They kept on pedalling through the pools of blood spilled along the road. Everywhere there was panic. Lying in a ditch, in the middle of a throng of refugees, Alberto was no longer afraid to die. The others around him gave him courage, he who had worried so often about death. If someone had to die, he was prepared to do so, instead of someone else. In four days they had covered only three hundred kilometres. They followed the general movement and headed away from the road to Bordeaux. They arrived in Moulins, but the next afternoon the Germans occupied the city. It was all over, escape was no longer possible, so Alberto decided to return to Paris immediately. If he was going to be a prisoner, he might as well be one in his own studio. The return journey was even more horrific. On the road there were cars, corpses, piles of abandoned luggage, a bearded man's severed head, a woman's arm with a bracelet of green stones still around her wrist, the bloated carcasses of horses. The stench was unbearable. They had spent the first night in a field near the road; the smell of bodies was so strong that they could not sleep. They set off again and found me sleeping outside the door. That was it. So what was I doing there?

The question had come too late. All I could think of was what they had told me.

Had Maman bought an emerald green bracelet?

Had Papa let his beard grow?

I was panicked. And anyway, what could I tell him after all the horrors he had just described? 'As for me, I haven't seen a single dead body. But I did just get thrown out by your friend, who kept me locked up for six months and neglected to tell me that the Germans were invading, you see, "It wouldn't be good for the baby..." I wasn't aware of anything going on, the only thing that mattered was my baby.' 'What baby?' 'Ah, yes, what baby! Well, the baby I made for her, for goodness' sake! Her name is Louise. But if you go and see her, she will tell you that it's her child, not mine, that I am completely mad and that I am trying to take it from her, that I've always been jealous of her. And if you ask around, all her friends, everyone, will tell you that I'm lying, that they saw she was pregnant all right.'

I couldn't tell him. What if he didn't believe me? I closed my eyes. If the Germans had just landed, perhaps I didn't give birth. Perhaps it was all shock. A traumatic experience. The discrepancy between my sensations and everyone else's was so great that I had begun to question my own experience. But the pain in my breasts was proof that yes, Louise did exist. So what should I have done? Show Alberto that my breasts were running with milk? Open my thighs so that he could see not the bloody roads he had just fled along, but a sight that was unsavoury all the same. To be honest, I didn't even think of it. Had Maman bought an emerald green bracelet? Had Papa let his beard grow? I had to get home, as quickly as possible.

I asked Alberto to lend me his bicycle. But he didn't want me to go on my own. It was too dangerous, and I was so pale. Did I feel all right?

How could he know that I no longer felt any pain. That I wouldn't see a thing. Not even the pigs rummaging through the dead bodies. That I wouldn't be afraid of anything. That my daughter had been taken from me, and my parents might be dead. I waited until he was asleep and then I fled. I would return his bicycle to him some day. He needed it less than I did. He had found his statues. I had to find my parents.

Louise was born on 16 May 1940.
I was born on 28 June 1940.

I was terrified these letters might be about me.

But my father had not been a journalist, and after the war he took over a printing press.

It was true that my grandparents had died before I was born, but I was not the only person on earth who did not know her grandparents. My child would not know hers, either.

And above all I had a brother, my beloved Pierre, the finest proof of all that my mother was not infertile.

I was having dinner with Nicolas that evening, seeing him again for the first time after so many weeks. I would tell him this story, he'd have a good laugh at me. You're forever making up stories, he would say.

Would I find the courage to tell him that these days, it was more like I was making a child?

I would not be able to hide it from him much longer, my baggiest jumpers would soon no longer be baggy enough. If he was hoping to bed a woman with a flat stomach, he was bound to be disappointed. For men, pregnancy means, first and foremost, the body of a woman who is now beyond their reach.

My father was sitting in the kitchen. When I came in, he sprang to his feet, but it wasn't me he had been expecting. Maman had disappeared. He had been all round the village and had not found a trace of her. He was desperate. She must have fled, like the others. When he came home everything was upside down, those fleeing had ransacked everything, even the rabbit hutches. He had been back in N. for two weeks.

On 3 June 1940, the guards had thrown them into the prison courtyard. The government didn't want them to fall into German hands. The Germans would have released them for sure. Ever since the Treaty of Non-Aggression between Germany and the Soviet Union, the Communists had been in the Boches' good books. They were being moved to another prison, they had to walk quickly, the guards were hitting them, shouting at them. It was late morning, they were on their way through Paris, when a guard suddenly pushed him out of the group and told him to get the hell out of there and fast, opportunity never knocks twice at anyone's door. They had let him go, and he still could not fathom why, but he was free, that was all that mattered.

His story made no sense to me at all. Not for one instant had I imagined that my parents might become separated. That Maman might be one of those corpses I had pedalled past as fast as I could in my haste to get home.

'Your parents are fine.' Madame M.'s news had never varied. Jacques too was a filthy liar: supposedly he'd been looking out for them.

If she had told me my father was in prison, I would have come home immediately to be with Maman. She knew that. Nothing could have stopped me. Neither her nor the pregnancy.

I had been right to find their silence odd. I had thought my father was being resentful; he was a prisoner. I had thought that Maman must be spending her days defending me. But she was struggling with herself, to keep from writing to me, not to spoil 'my stay in Collioure', which she imagined must be wonderful. She must have kept telling herself that my coming home sooner would not bring back her husband. That is why she hadn't written. She figured it would not surprise me unduly. My father had been very clear on the matter the day I left.

Now Madame M.'s lies were revealed to me in all their monstrous cruelty. The trouble she had gone to in order to have Louise left me in no doubt as to the trouble she would go to in order to keep her. The prospect terrified me. My father a prisoner. The Germans victorious. Paris occupied. What else had she hidden from me? What else was I about to discover?

But my father, too, had lied to me. After the Pact, he swore to me that he had left the Party. Why hadn't he kept his promise? He would not have been arrested. Maman would not have disappeared. He would have protected her. I suddenly started screaming at him. Stalin, Stalin, all he'd cared about was Stalin. He must be happy now that Stalin's new comrades might have killed Maman! Oh sorry, perhaps one ought to see that as an honour, after all?

'Hold your tongue!'

My father slapped me and dragged me by the hair over to his night table. He opened the drawer. His Party card was there, torn into pieces.

'I didn't lie to you. I told the gendarmes those days were over, but they just laughed at me and said I couldn't fool them, just tearing up a card didn't mean a thing. Besides, they didn't give a toss what I was today, I'd been a filthy Red, a traitor to the homeland, that was enough. That's how it happened! Defeatist words. Two years of prison without remission, a fine of two thousand francs. There was nothing I could do to keep those bastards from carting me off. And all because at the café I'd said that the blokes on the Maginot line were good-for-nothing layabouts who'd rather play a game of cards than work...'

My father suddenly stopped talking. Given the way he was looking at me, I prayed he'd go no further. That he would not say what I knew he was going to say.

'Christ almighty, girl, wake up! You think you have nothing to do with this whole bloody business? It's all well and good to pin the blame on others, but don't you go forgetting that if you hadn't gone off with your ladi-da lady, your mother would never have ended up all on her own...'

For the second time in my life I saw my father cry. The first time was when the Soviets signed the Pact.

I had tried to bury my responsibility beneath his. But I knew it was my fault. I had left of my own free will; he'd only got caught up in a political game he had no control over. Communism had become the public enemy number one, and if you couldn't go to war, you had to make a war.

Night was falling.

After a long while my father placed his hand on my shoulder. The electricity had been cut, so he was going to get a candle. Now that there were two of us, it was worthwhile using the candle. He said this and gave me one of those little winks of his I knew so well. Sadder than usual. But a wink all the same. And besides, we had to celebrate my return, there wasn't much to eat, but we'd find something. He squeezed my shoulder, hard. It was his last act of tenderness towards me. He asked me if at least I'd been painting all this time, if I hadn't already outgrown his easel. He thought I'd grown. I didn't have the strength to reply. He didn't have the strength to go and look for the candle. He sat back down and we stayed there. Without talking. In the dark. If he only knew how much I had grown. I could tell he knew nothing about Louise.

I waited until he had gone to bed to open Maman's trunk of material. If she hadn't taken my letters with her, this is where I would find them, on top of the bolts of material, next to her Bible. There was no material any more, no Bible; but my letters were there. Bound with a white ribbon. All of them, except the last one. The only one that was of the slightest importance. The one where I told her everything.

That was when I realised that Sophie had not posted it.

If Maman had known about me, about the baby, she wouldn't have left. I am sure of that. She would have waited for me. I wasn't sleepy, I needed some air. I needed to walk. My body was aching. I felt wornout. Drained. But my mind was seething. War, this was war, the real thing. I tried not to listen to the howling of the cats and dogs roaming everywhere in the village. People had abandoned them during their flight. And there were cows mooing in pain; no one had milked them for days. Like me. My breasts hurt. Milk was oozing onto my shirt. I collapsed outside the gate to L'Escalier. I had made my way there, without thinking. I wept and wept. I called out to Maman.

For weeks we waited for her to return. I prayed with all my strength that she was all right. That she had found shelter somewhere. Every day there were people returning to the village. But there was never anyone who had seen her.

After some time had gone by we did the same thing a lot of people had done, we put a notice in the newspaper. It was the only thing left to do. But we didn't really know what to write. We knew nothing. We didn't know where she had gone. Or when. Or how she was dressed. I tried to work that out. Maman didn't have very many dresses; I could have figured out which one was missing. But when I stood before her wobbly wardrobe, I realised I no longer knew the clothes she had. For months I hadn't paid the slightest attention to the woman I now claimed to love with all my soul. You could not blame life for taking something from you when you hardly even noticed it any more.

If we wanted to be in with a chance of finding her, though, we had to put something in our notice. So we put her name. Her age. Her white hair. That much we were sure about. The beauty spot she had in the hollow at the back of her neck, right at the roots of her hair. And even her broken tooth, the right-hand canine. Maybe her Bible. We couldn't be sure about that, either. She might have left with it then lost it along the way. And above all – above all – we would refund any telegram expenses so that we could be sure that money would not prevent any news of her from reaching us. Then we waited. Until that Friday, 30 November 1940.

I will always remember the date, Louis, it was not long after your return. I was also worried about you. You cannot imagine how happy I was. For the first time in all those long months, I said to myself, 'It's going to be all right. It's going to be all right. Louis is home. Now everything will be all right. Maman will come home, too.' And then we got the telegram. The only news of her that we did not want to get.

```
regret to inform stop eugénie gallois
dead  stop  bombing  stop  personal
belongings to follow by post stop
```

The doubt. Unbearable. A few more days. And then the package. Her Bible. Her wedding ring. A little bit of money. And the thimble I had given her and which she always had with her. The certainty of it. Maman was dead.

We had never had much to say to each other, my father and I, and from that day on, it was finished for good. I handed him Maman's ring. He threw it back in my face.

'It's a living woman I married, not a dead one.'

That was the end of my family life. Never again would there be the three of us, never again could we be just the two of us, either. Strangers meeting over a meal, that was all we were. And even eating didn't release any meaning, as we faced off pitifully across the table.

My father had taken in a stray dog, and he'd talk to it, short commands like sit, lie down, give me your paw, good dog...Those were the only words that came out of his mouth. I was there, but it was as if he had erased me from his life. He seemed to have got used to it. I hadn't. He held me responsible for Maman's death and I couldn't say anything. In a way he was right. I had the impression that nothing I did could ever be as good as the way she had done it. Her memory was everywhere. I couldn't stay there. With my father looking at me but not seeing me, my remorse was slowly killing me. And I had to live, for Louise's sake. That is why I went away again. Forgive me, Louis, forgive me for leaving the village without saying goodbye. But if I had come to see you, I would have told you everything. And I didn't want to get you mixed up in it. I had only one thought in my mind: to get my child back.

I don't know how I managed to read to the end of that letter.

I finished it – drained, stunned, as I repeated the same gesture again and again, of running my finger over the hollow in the nape of my neck, at the roots of my hair.

Over my beauty spot.

Annie had left me outside the entrance to the municipal baths, but not before she had told me several times that she would be right back. I waited for her in the café opposite, still shocked by what she had just told me.

I wondered what she had done to Sophie to 'make her pay' for not sending the letter; there was so much hatred in her eyes when she said it. What I imagined was nowhere near the truth, and I will be sorry all my life for having been the cause of it.

A quarter of an hour after she had left me Annie tapped on the windowpane by the table where I was sitting. She was smiling; she had put on a bit of lipstick. She was beautiful, even more beautiful than she had been in the village. Her husband was a lucky man. It was strange for me to see her resorting to artifice; she really was a woman now. But I too had become a man, and to see the proof that one is growing older is always a bit sad, even when one is young, and even when one is a man.

She motioned for to me to join her. She smelled good. She had heard about a restaurant where you could still find decent things to eat, and she was about to continue her story when I interrupted her. I had to confess to her now; afterwards it would be too late.

'I sent you that telegram. Your mother died before my eyes.'

Annie put down her fork, speechless.

At least I could try to restore some truth to this story riddled with lies. I could not tell her about the letter she had sent to her mother, but I had to tell her everything about the telegram.

When everyone was beginning to flee, my mother insisted I leave the village. She could not bear to think I might end up in the hands of the Germans, the way they had in 1914. If my father had not been at the front, he would have told me to leave too, of that she was sure. She would stay behind in the village with my sisters, that was her duty. She closed the haberdashery in order to teach the village children – one fine morning Mademoiselle E. had simply failed to turn up. She had vanished into thin air like so many others.

My mother kept telling me that for me it was different: I wasn't running away, like all those cowards; I was leaving in order to defend us if things got worse, and it was my duty to obey the orders of the authorities. 'All boys of over sixteen must avoid capture from the enemy.'

I was to set off with four friends who had also decided to leave. We didn't really know where to go, we wanted at least to get to the other side of the Seine, to get away from the Germans; we still thought the army would stop them before then.

I had promised Annie's mother that I would pop in to say goodbye. She was sitting on the same stool in the hallway as on the afternoon when she had told me she didn't know how to read. She was wearing her coat, and between her feet she had a small suitcase. She was waiting for me. If I still didn't know where to go, she did. To Collioure, to join Annie. Did I want to come with her? She was leaving, no matter what. There was no point trying to make her change her mind, the most recent bombing attacks had convinced her. She would not stay another minute to wait for the Boches' flame-throwers to come and singe her bottom, particularly as now my mother had closed the haberdashery, and her 'intelligent eyes' were leaving her as well. That's what she called me, her 'intelligent eyes'. Should we say goodbye there and then, or did I want to go with her to look for Annie?

I couldn't abandon her, she wouldn't be able to cope on her own, nor could I impose her on my friends, so I didn't join them. We could always go a little bit of the way together, as far as the station.

People were shouting, fighting, trampling on each other, because it was those who managed to get on the train who'd be able to flee; the Germans might show up at any minute. They were bombing the rail convoys relentlessly. I decided to take the main road; a moving crowd seemed less dangerous than a stampeding crowd.

We found ourselves among a group of good village souls. They had piled everything higgledy-piggledy onto their carts: supplies, furniture, canary cages, rabbit hutches, two old women and a child. They kindly cleared a spot for Annie's mother so she could sit down. We inched our way along, followed by a few tireless goats. Everyone was afraid.

On the third day, we went through a little abandoned village. Outside the pharmacy a man in rags was meticulously arranging medicine bottles according to colour, and every time he saw someone, he said, 'Just a little shot, Monsieur Thingmajig, just a little shot.' And on the square were a man and a woman, also in rags, and espadrilles, and they answered 'Napoleon' and 'Joan of Arc' when we asked them their names.

They were lunatics who had escaped from a hospice because the nurses had abandoned them as they fled. Suddenly this particular Joan of Arc started screaming, hiding her head with her hands.

'Aeroplanes! Aeroplanes!'

Black dots were in fact emerging from the clouds. A squadron of several dozen Stukas with their wings in a W formation and their sirens sounding were headed in our direction. Everyone panicked.

'Bloody hell, you're the ones they're aiming for, take off that uniform, quick!'

One of the men was screaming at a group of fleeing soldiers who had joined us.

'You fucking bastard soldiers! Why don't you stick together and fight each other instead of hanging around with civilians and landing us with all these fucking Stukas.'

They would have come to blows for sure if those 'fucking Stukas' had not come straight at us. I shouted at Annie's mother to get down off the cart. I tried to make my way over to her. She was walking as fast as she could but she couldn't run. I heard the whistling of machine-gun fire. I could see the ground exploding all around us. The bombing was terrifying. When it was calm again at last, and once they'd recovered their wits, everyone immediately looked for their loved ones. I was so relieved, her mother was in the ditch a few metres from me, safe and sound, reciting her act of contrition. Everywhere else there was nothing but screaming. Napoleon and Joan of Arc were writhing on the ground in fear, like lunatics indeed. And in the middle of all the shouts were even more terrible cries, a little girl with her mother lying in a pool of blood at her feet, dead. Behind me there was a strange noise, like tiny bursts of machine-gun fire. I turned around: it was a swarm of bees, circling madly, relentlessly, around their hive which had been crushed in the attack. It was a terrifying vision, a scene from the Apocalypse.

Then suddenly I heard new cries, more animated, more intense. Out of nowhere – no doubt he'd escaped from his paddock thanks to the bombs – a horse had just broken through the hedge between us, and it was as if he had gone mad. People were running in every direction to get away from him. When I looked around again for Annie's mother, she was no longer next to me. She was comforting the little girl whose mother was lying at her feet. The horse was headed straight for them. It all happened so fast, there was nothing I could do. Nor did she have the time to react. When she saw the horse it was too late. She lay over the little girl to protect her with her body, and the horse's hoof struck her right in the back of the skull. She died instantly.

*

'I hoped I would never see you again, I felt so guilty. But when I went back to N., you were there, back from your "trip"with Madame M. I didn't recognise you any more, you looked so tired, so sad. I read your notice in *La Gazette* every day, and finally I replied. With this telegram. Because I was too much of a coward to tell you to your face. Because I didn't want to become the person who told you that your mother had died: I know that once someone tells you such a terrible piece of news you can never see them as anyone but a bearer of bad news. I did not manage to protect her. Please forgive me.'

'It wasn't your fault.'

Annie was in shock, but she seemed to be thinking about something.

'What day did you say you left?'

'The twenty-third of May.'

'That's what I thought. If Sophie had posted my letter the morning after the birth, like she had promised me she would, my mother would have got it and she would never have left, she would have waited for me. You see, it's not really your fault.'

How much guiltier could Annie make me feel?

I suddenly felt the waiter tapping me on the shoulder.

'I'm sorry, but I have to ask you youngsters to leave now, we're closing up.'

It was already a quarter to midnight; the time had flown by. We were the last customers, the chairs were already on top of the tables. As the door to the restaurant was closing behind us, the loudspeakers on the police cars blared their message into the street.

'Attention, attention, any individuals found in the street after midnight will be taken to the police station and held there until five o'clock in the morning.'

Whether we went to my place or Annie's, it would still take us longer than fifteen minutes, and she preferred to come to my place. Of course! Her husband must be at home. And what if she didn't love him any more? The thought suddenly crossed my mind.

We ran as far as the métro; I have such a vibrant memory of that mad dash. We ran, looked at each other, ran, looked at each other. And once we were in the métro, out of breath, red in the face, we were overcome by an irrepressible and inappropriate fit of laughter, one of those childhood fits from when we were still 'those inseparable kids', as my father used to call us… like those lovebirds you must always buy in pairs, otherwise they will die.

When we got out of the métro it was after midnight. And we had at least five hundred metres left to get to my place. We mustn't be caught. The wooden soles of Annie's shoes made such a racket that it felt as if, with each step she took, every German guard in Paris must be about to descend upon us. I told her to climb onto my back. She didn't want to, no doubt out of a sense of female vanity. I insisted.

'Do you know what happened the other night near the Luxembourg Gardens? At twenty minutes past nine?'

'No.'

'A Jew killed a German soldier, ripped his guts out

and ate his heart.'

Annie was giving me an odd look.

'What are you talking about?'

'You know perfectly well that Germans don't have hearts, that Jews don't eat pork, and that at twenty minutes past nine everyone is listening to the British radio. Feel my soles.'

I was used to dealing with the curfew: my soles were made of felt. I walked right down the middle of the street to avoid the soldiers patrolling the pavement on either side; I had already fooled them any number of times. If I happened upon a group of guards I would stop and wait for them to move on; we simply had to do the same thing now. In the dark they could not see a thing. Annie climbed on my back; I could tell she was proud of me.

I tried not to panic. Evidently, whoever was writing these letters wanted to make me believe that he was talking about me. But who could want to do this to me?

Other than the men in my life, no one knew about my beauty spot: I have long hair and never tie it back. As for author-lovers, I've always tried to avoid them, I have to live with writers all day long, so to have one in my bed, no thanks! Nicolas said that no beauty spot had ever been more deserving of its name, and he was very fond of it. He would have done better to be fond of me.

Our dinner was an utter fiasco. Apparently that word is supposed to apply to sexual relations. But this wasn't far off, same difference. I should just call the baby 'fiasco' in honour of its father.

Nicolas was muttering between clenched teeth. He accused me of trying to have a baby behind his back. He should have expected as much: at my age, that's all women think about, their biological clock.

I got up and said that Cinderella had to get home, that she wouldn't lose her shoe, and that he could just go fuck himself. Just like he had fucked me in order to make this baby.

What with Nicolas and all these letters, I hadn't eaten much for several days. But I had to get something down my throat for the baby's sake. Now I was even beginning to sound like those letters.

I found two slices of ham in the fridge, that was already something. Maman always said you could tell when people were depressed because they ate straight out of the fridge, so I went and sat back down at my desk, but not on the side where I work, the other side, closer to the kitchen, not so much to try and get comfortable but simply to stay off my feet, and above all keep my nose out of the fridge.

And that is when it came to me. Which just goes to show that it is always a good thing in life to change your point of view; I mean your perspective, not your opinion.

From that point of view a squadron of Stukas was in plain sight, their wings shaped like Ws.

While I was reading I had automatically scribbled the letter W on the back of the envelope, but from where I was sitting those Stukas were not very frightening any more, they were no more than an army of the letter M staring at me, inoffensively.

Madame M.

I turned the envelope upside down.

M W M W.

And what if this were a hidden initial?

What if Madame M., that monster the guy was describing to me week after week, was actually Madame W.?

A Madame Werner, for example.

An Elisabeth Werner, like my mother. Well, 'my mother…'

I felt sick to my stomach. I went and threw up.

Could that really be my life? My life from before memory?

I didn't want to believe it, but I could not ignore it. These letters were giving too much away, with too many details. I had to find the author, dammit, I had to have it out with him.

He had told me nothing about himself, but if I went back over all the letters I'd got, right from the start, I was bound to find some sort of clue that would lead me to him.

Deeply uneasy, I waited until the following Tuesday, hoping he would come out with the last word, but I was afraid of it, all the same.

I could not go as quickly as on other nights – Annie slowed me down, not because she was a burden, but because of who she was. The satisfaction of feeling her weight upon my back, her body against mine, troubled me and overwhelmed me with desire. It was sweet, so sweet to know she could not get off my back and go away from me. I could have walked like that all night, the two of us now one. If that morning of October 1943 someone had told me that after midnight Annie would be on my back, I would never have believed it. With my hands under her buttocks, I walked as silently as possible, while I recalled the day I thought I had lost her for ever.

'Annie was not even at the funeral. Her own mother, can you imagine?'

My sister, who normally loved to dwell on the slightest scrap of gossip and give her opinion at least three times over, went no further in this instance than a simple statement of fact. Death had become too palpable for anyone to delight in talking about it, even her.

The fact remained that no one could accept that a daughter had not gone to her own mother's funeral. I could understand it – what was the point of this final encounter where there was no one there to greet you any more? And for Annie it was even worse, her mother's body was not even there. In that church there was nothing but a dizzying absence.

Annie had left N. the day of the mass in memory of her mother. I knew that she was not just fleeing from the mass, but that she had left town, and I was determined to go and look for her.

I had no difficulty finding their address in Paris. At the post office a man my age passed on the information with an odd smile. At the time I did not understand why. He seemed to know the place very well, or at least the neighbourhood. There was an art gallery in the street perpendicular to hers, go past that and then take the first right. Number 65.

I rang the bell.

It was Madame M. who opened. She was holding the baby in her arms. I could not believe it, Annie's baby. I could not take my eyes off her. She tightened her hold on the child.

No, Annie was not there, unfortunately, she had had no news of her whatsoever, but she had not entirely given up hope she might hear something someday. She was not angry with her, no, she knew that love can often lead one to abandon a friendship, at least in the beginning, and frankly, who was she to talk, it was exactly the same with a baby. Annie must be with him right now, as we were speaking. He must have had the good fortune to avoid being taken prisoner, and they must have managed to find one another; Annie had been waiting so impatiently for his letters.

Who was she talking about, for God's sake?

Oh, I'm so sorry! She thought that Annie must have mentioned her young man to me, but it's true that it's not always easy for a young woman to talk about one young man to another young man, if I could see what she meant...There was nothing particularly unusual about their story. During the time she had spent with Annie, the young woman had fallen in love, his name was Henri. Annie had offered to adopt a soldier, to be a sort of war godmother to him, and as was often the case, she had ended up falling in love with the fellow, a good lad to judge from what Annie had let her read of his letters. In any case a good-looking one, very good-looking, to judge from the photograph that Annie had shown her. She must be married by now, that's just how Annie was, an all or nothing sort of girl, but I must know that already since I was her friend...Her childhood friend, was that it?

'Yes, that was it.' I heard my voice slurring. 'Thank you, Madame, I am sorry to have bothered you.'

And then I looked at the infant one last time. 'Goodbye, Louise.'

As I said goodbye to that little creature I knew I was saying goodbye to Annie.

This was no longer any of my business, I had to forget now, too: if Annie had decided to abandon her child to this woman, I could not stand in her way. All the more so because I knew Louise would be happy, that Madame M. would love her with all the vehemence of an illegitimate love, of the type that can be lost from one day to the next, for the law of blood does not make such love everlasting.

I had arrived at the M. residence with the confidence of a saviour; I was leaving in a state of agitation, as I had been spurned. Annie was in love with another man, and I was ashamed that I had not thought of it sooner. A soldier: it was normal, manhood was to be found at the front, love as well. It was all over. I knew Annie well enough to realise that if there were a man who had managed to charm her, he would become her entire life.

I stopped outside the art gallery, the one the postal employee had mentioned to me, and the paintings in the window reminded me of Annie's. But as I looked up to see the name of the shop, I suddenly understood what it actually concealed. The size of the number left no doubt: as required by law, it was larger than all the other numbers on the street. It was a brothel.

Now I knew why the postal employee had had such a lewd smile on his face, and recalling his deliberately comical expression made me smile in turn. From my reflection in the window I could see my face light up and become more pleasant, more handsome, perhaps not as good-looking as the soldier on the photograph, but not necessarily without beauty. If another woman's painting could make me think of Annie, some day another person, another laugh, another body would make me think of her and then I would be able to love again. I must smile, and go on smiling, and another woman would come. I remembered the little notice on display in the jaunty postal employee's window.

Help wanted.
Inquire first office on the right.

Why not? I had to begin my life somehow or other.

I kept on promising myself to forget Annie, when suddenly she reappeared in my life, obliterating in one second all the long labour of forgetting that I had imposed on myself for three years. I had buried her in a corner of my brain, as far away as possible. If I happened to think about her – Did she have a family with her handsome soldier? Did she ever think of the little girl she had abandoned? Did she ever think about me? – I did not let myself go. I liked my work. I liked my life. I did not like the times in which we were living, but I did what I could to fight back. No grand deeds of resistance, but what I could. At the post office I was, in some ways, in a good position to manoeuvre. I spent the first half of the day in the sorting room and the afternoon at the counter. Let's just say I did not make the Germans' job of censoring any easier.

It must have been around three o'clock, I had just come back from a break with Moustique, his real name was Maurice, but everyone called him Moustique, Mosquito, because he couldn't sit still. The first thing I saw was her hand, on a letter. At first I paid no attention, for I could not take my eyes off the envelope as I stared at the familiar handwriting. I don't know how many long seconds went by before I could look up.

I wanted no part of the scene that was about to unfold before my eyes. I was not ready to see her again, I was not strong enough to go on with my life afterwards as if nothing had happened. She was smiling at me. She must have seen the shadow of discontent pass over my face. Had I grimaced? Her smile lost some of its assurance.

'Hello, Louis.'

'Hello.'

'What a coincidence to find you here. By chance.'

'True enough.'

'How are you?'

'Fine.'

More than that I could not manage. I could not suddenly start chatting about this and that as if we had just parted the night before. She sensed this and, to make things worse, the people in the queue behind her were getting impatient. She said a hasty goodbye. I was devastated. It was the end, I could tell, the end of all the peace of mind I'd fought for, bit by bit, day after day, burying my memories. I hated her for coming back into my life like this without warning. I had to be stronger than her sudden apparition. I mustn't let her eat away at my existence any more. She had gone away without saying goodbye and, for three years, not a word. She had made her life, I had to go on with mine. I must stand by my resolve not to think about her, I had managed perfectly well only a few minutes earlier. Nothing need change.

That evening I was planning to see Joëlle, who was my girlfriend at the time. Nothing need change...

I broke up with her. No matter how I claimed it had nothing to do with Annie's sudden reappearance, no matter that for several weeks already I had been thinking that, true enough, Joëlle was not the right girl for me, I had not broken up with her for all that.

And what was supposed to happen did happen: I began to wait for her. Not the right girl for me, no. Of course not. Annie. Once I got into the habit of searching the queues for her face, all I did was look at the letters or packages that people shoved my way, for I was trying to recreate the circumstances of her appearance. But as always, Annie suddenly showed up when I least expected her.

One week later, that famous 4 October 1943, I found her waiting for me at the entrance, on the pavement, leaning against the wall.

That is how we had ended up walking to her place, where she made me a cup of chicory coffee, where she left me on my own while she returned the keys. That is how I ended up going with her to the municipal baths, and waiting for her in a café, before sharing a wonderful dinner, sad but wonderful. And that is how we now found ourselves walking along in that pleasantly awkward situation, where my wandering hands had never been so happy, even while remaining still.

I was roused abruptly from my thoughts by the sound of boots headed our way, rhythmic and aggressive. The voices were German, and Annie had heard them, too. She hugged me closer. I froze in the middle of the dark street, careful that no halo from a streetlamp might betray our presence. All we could do was wait. I could feel that Annie was squeezing me tighter and tighter, I thought it was fear, but it was her asthma, suddenly uncontrollable. She began to cough; it was terribly loud in the silence. There was barking and a jangling of metal: the soldiers trained their torch beams on us and then led us away.

After they had checked our papers they took us to the cells. The others who had been arrested that night stayed in the common room with the guards; they could even play cards while they waited until five o'clock. But Annie had been on my back when they found us, and the officers considered this to be a veritable conspiracy against German order, a crime that went beyond a simple failure to obey the curfew. I had not spoken out in our defence; it would be better if they forgot about us – it had not yet occurred to them to look under my shoes.

Our two cells were next to each other. The women on one side, the men on the other. A new school, and still the same rules. We were sitting on either side of the same wall. Annie kept saying we weren't in any danger: this had already happened to friends of hers and they had been released. Annie was so sweet. I did not want to frighten her. I did not want to tell her that her friends had simply been lucky that there had been no acts of violence against the Germans on the night they were imprisoned. Otherwise her friends who'd got off so lightly would have been summarily lined up before the firing squad at five o'clock in the morning, in reprisal. I did not want to tell her that what had not happened to her friends could well happen to us.

'Louis?'

'Yes.'

'I didn't go into your post office just by chance.'

Apparently she still had more things to reveal.

'I knew you worked there. Your mother told me,

when I went back to look for you in the village. I also went to see my father. From a distance. It's strange, all the people I love, right now I have to watch them from a distance as they get on with their lives. I didn't want it to be like that with you. My father seemed smaller somehow. I hope it was the distance and not old age. I didn't go up to him because my life was a mess just then. But now things are different, aren't they? Louis?'

'Yes.'

'Can we go back together to see him?'

'Of course.'

'And you'll help me get Louise back.'

'As soon as we get out of here.'

'No, not like that. I want to do things properly, for Louise's sake. And for yours, too.'

'What do you want to do?'

'We…do you remember when we used to play "dot-dash"?'

And then I heard her murmuring, very quietly, not to wake up the guards, reviving the code we used to use as children so that no one would understand us.

Dash dash (M)

Dot dash (A)

Dot dash dot (R)

Dot dash dot (R)

Dash dot dash dash (Y)

There we were. Her handsome soldier, we would get there eventually, I didn't want to deal with it, but I couldn't avoid the subject indefinitely. At least I had to acknowledge her tactfulness in telling me about him.

'And why hasn't he helped you get your daughter back?'

'Who?'

'Your husband.'

'But I don't have a husband.'

'You're not married?'

'That's what I just said.'

I was flabbergasted. I had been so convinced of the contrary. And what about her ring?

'But it's Maman's ring. I told you earlier that Papa threw it in my face when we received the package. Well, I mean, your package...I kept it.'

I felt extremely embarrassed and extremely happy.

'So...there is no one in your life?'

I remember very well how long her silence was. I thought she wanted to reply using dot-dash, but could not remember the code. But that wasn't it; her voice was choked with emotion.

'I loved someone, but it's all over.'

I heard her sobbing then. I didn't know what to say. I was still in shock. No more handsome soldier.

'Don't cry, Annie.'

'Don't you think, Louis, that in other people's lives there is the past which matters and the past which doesn't matter?'

'Of course.'

That must not have been the answer she expected. She continued to cry; I thought it was because of the handsome soldier, but it was because of my silence.

She murmured, 'So you don't want to?'

Only then did I understand what I had failed to grasp before, because I had hoped for it so much, and I stammered, as intimidated as I would have been had the priest been right there with us.

Dash dot dash dash
Dot
Dot dot dot
Must I translate my reply?
YES.

'That year at the centre of the world there was me, and there was Annie. All around us lots of things were happening that I couldn't care less about. In Germany, Hitler had become chancellor of the Reich, and the Nazi party exercised single party rule. Brecht and Einstein had fled while Dachau was being built. It is the naïve pretension of childhood to think one can be sheltered from history.'

That year had been 1933, I had checked.

If Louis was twelve then, today he would be fifty-four, more or less the same age as Madame Merleau.

Louis was his real name, and Annie was her real name, too, I could tell. The man was not lying, he was just hiding one aspect of reality, the part that could hurt.

So I had to find a certain Louis, fifty-four years old. That was a good start, but I wouldn't get far with it.

The only solution seemed to be to find the village of 'N.'. There, too, I had the feeling that the initial was the real one, no need to turn it every which way, it hid no secrets other than the letters that should follow.

In the village there was bound to be someone who could give me the names of the doctor or the haberdashery owner from that era, and if there was no one to inform me, there was always the town hall. I would go through the registers, and once I had the name, it would be child's play to find my way back to Louis. And then I could look him straight in the eye and force him to tell me what he knew, and we would find out soon enough whether his story held together or not.

'Roughly two weeks later I had further proof that something was not quite right. This time it was her husband's car that was parked in the drive. As a rule he had already left for his newspaper office by the time I arrived.'

'N.' must be less than two hours' drive from Paris, otherwise Monsieur M. – my father? – would not have been able to come and go on a daily basis between his house and his office. It seemed a long way, but it was feasible, and I had to start as far out as possible.

'Jacques had stayed behind at L'Escalier...He was the one who came up once a week to Paris with news of my parents, but I never saw him, I could only hear his voice.'

If I relied on this expression – coming *up* to Paris – I could eliminate the north. And concentrate, therefore, on the region to the south, east and west of Paris. I could always return to it later if I didn't find anything.

And perhaps Jacques, the very zealous Jacques, would still be there looking after L'Escalier, in spite of all the years gone by, never giving up hope that his masters might return some day. Perhaps he would know where to find Louis. He might be able to provide all the missing explanations.

I went out and bought a road map, and drew a semi-circle with the dividers: two hours from Paris, to the south. It still left me with a vast area to search.

Night after night I studied the map by the light of my bedside lamp. It was killing my eyesight. There were so many villages beginning with N, it would take me months to visit them all. It was discouraging. I looked at the lamp. The first night Nicolas came to my house I had changed the bulb for a weaker, more 'romantic' one. I would have done better to leave the big fat white bulb that was so unflattering: perhaps we wouldn't have made love and at least I'd be able to read this fucking road map that was dancing before my eyes. I looked at my belly, feeling uncomfortable the way I did whenever an unpleasant thought crossed my mind; forgive me, baby, of course I'm happy you exist.

There was a sudden shrill ring at the door.

Nicolas? Look, my village too begins with an N.

'It's us! Open up, Camille, we have loads of food… and booze!'

It was just like my girlfriends to show up without warning. I hadn't told them anything yet, I wasn't strong enough to confront them. But now that I'd made my decision, now that Nicolas had said what he had to say, I'd be able to tell them as well. I was glad they had come. We would be able to talk about it, they would surely reproach me for embarking on this adventure all by myself, but they would not spare Nicolas either, and it would do me good to hear them say bad things about him.

They were overjoyed for my sake, they would be there, they would help me, had I already chosen a name? Three pairs of wildly enthusiastic hands wandered over my tummy. My girlfriends: they are the best thing that has happened to me in life. You have to pick them well, you lose a few along the way, but the ones I have kept are the most wonderful girls on the planet.

Two of us were not drinking champagne: me, for obvious reasons, and Charlotte, for no other reasons than her palate. No, really, she said, the only thing she liked about the Champagne region were the timber-frame churches.

'The *what*?'

'The timber-frame churches. They're churches made all of wood, all lovely and warm, like chalets, you only find them in Champagne, a dozen or so in all.'

Charlotte always knew how to catch us out.

'I was overcome by a certain sweet feeling, and I rediscovered with pleasure the smell of wood that was so peculiar to that church.'

Oh my God, there it was! I had the missing clue.

The village of N. must be in Champagne. It was less than two hours from Paris by car, to the southwest; it corresponded perfectly.

Charlotte never found out what she did for me.

And while they were having a field day bad-mouthing Nicolas-that-filthy-bastard, I looked at my friends with all the love I felt for them. Louis would not get away from me now.

First thing the next morning I asked Mélanie, the young intern, to look up the names of all the villages where one could find timber-frame churches.

When she brought me the list, there was not a single one that began with the letter N.

It was Tuesday, and no matter how many times I read and reread the letters, I could not unlock the past.

At five o'clock sharp I heard the key turn in the lock of Annie's cell. We were free; our lives would not be used to compensate for the misdeeds of others. It was still pitch black outside and when we left the premises it was drizzling. We headed for my house. We wouldn't really have time to get any sleep but we'd be able to rest, if she wanted. Annie came closer and put her arm around my waist; I put mine on her shoulder. We had never walked like this together; I felt invincible.

Moustique didn't wake up. We went into my room and lay down on my bed. When I tried to kiss her, determined to make love to her, Annie gently pushed me away. She sat up against the headboard. She wanted to do it with her husband, she said, not with a man 'like the others'. But it wasn't a matter of making me wait, we could get married that very evening, if I liked. Father André would do it even if we showed up without warning. Father André was our village priest. And after that, she would be happy, her mind at rest. We would love each other as man and wife, and we would go and get Louise as man and wife, and as her parents, if I was all right with that, if I agreed to play the role.

I looked at her; she was unfathomable. I hadn't known she was so pious. Already the previous day the crucifix in her room had surprised me.

Annie suddenly got up. She burst out laughing, but ever so gently. She began to go round in circles humming, 'here is a dance for my fiancé', lifting her jumper as she moved, hiding and revealing her beautiful breasts, naked beneath the jumper. And then she froze there before me and huddled against me and asked me to hold her closely. She would come for me at two o'clock, when I finished work, and afterwards we would go directly to the church, would that be all right?

This was wonderful! But how did she know I finished work at two o'clock? I was about to ask her, when Moustique came into the room shouting at the top of his lungs in his usual way, 'Breakfast is ready, comrade!' 'Comrades,' he added, when he saw Annie. Her presence at my side did not surprise him for one second; on the contrary.

'Well, well! It looks like you finally found each other, the two of you.'

I had my answer. Annie had asked Moustique about me.

Moustique, the fellow with the lewd smile. The day I began work at the post office he had offered me a room: his best friend, who had been renting it, had been taken prisoner, and while Moustique was happy to wait for him, in the meantime he needed the money. I could stay until he came back. But three years had gone by, and he hadn't come back, and neither Moustique nor I saw any reason to change our arrangement. He was messy, I was tidy. Rather than fight about it, I would pick up his mess, and he would add a bit of mess to my life, since I was too timorous to do it on my own. I always met my girlfriends through Moustique. You might have thought we didn't live in the same town: I simply could not see the pretty girls, but for him it was as if he created them. There was not one of his conquests who wasn't charming, and luckily for me they all had friends who were just as charming. There are people who are gifted at this sort of thing, able to find beauty no matter where they are. When I asked him how he met these women he always said, 'Just horsing about.' Since the death of Annie's mother I could not stand that expression, but no matter how often I told him so he always forgot. He wasn't being cruel, that's just the way Moustique was.

'You see, if you know how to horse about you can find a lot of women, but not a thoroughbred like her. Now I understand why you never noticed my women.'

That's what he said while Annie was in the bathroom. We had had a very lively breakfast the three of us, full of laughter. And then I had to go to work. Moustique had the day off, as did Annie, or so she said. She walked with me as far as the post office, and to say goodbye she kissed me on the cheek close to my lips, murmuring, 'I will see you later, my almost husband.' I shall always remember.

I spent the morning looking at the time, raging against the slowness of the clock hands. At three minutes to two I put on my pea jacket and went out. Annie wasn't there. I didn't worry, I was early. But at half past she wasn't there either. I waited for her until three o'clock, pacing the same few feet of pavement, not knowing what I was supposed to think. I was furious. Where had she got to? Did she intend to let me down my whole life? At three twenty I was pounding on the door to her room. No one. I turned the knob. The door opened, it wasn't locked. I thought of waiting for her there, but it was as if the sculpture on the table – the 'Invisible Object' – were staring at me. And in the hands of the woman who only yesterday had seemed to be holding nothing but the empty space, there was a sheet of paper. I went over; on the paper was a hasty sketch.

A drawing which, although I had never seen it, was uncannily familiar.

It was a picture of a little boy playing with a doll by the side of a lake. A pile of stones next to him.

And in the lake, Annie had written a sentence, seven words I wish I had never shared with her.

'Here, at last, I am at peace...'

I had once told Annie all about the painter Elisabeth Vigée-Lebrun. This was the epitaph she had carved onto her tombstone at the end of her sad life.

It was as if I had been struck by lightning. I couldn't understand a thing. What had happened between this morning, when she had painted such a radiant future for us, and this letter, and this drawing, which made me fear the worst?

My thoughts were racing, but I couldn't move, until I felt something beneath my fingers, like a low relief etching, and I turned the paper over: letters had been cut out and stuck to the page.

IT ISN'T NICE TO GO HIDING THINGS
WHO'S GOING TO TELL
YOUR NEW BOYFRIEND
THAT HE'S SLEEPING
WITH A WHORE

My blood ran cold. Annie, a whore?

She must have received the anonymous letter that morning.

I scrambled down the steps four at a time, leapt on my bicycle and pedalled as fast as I could.

So she knew my secret of the porcelain dolls: she must have caught me at it on one of the drowning days.

I didn't stop, I tore along. I shouted so people would get off the pavement and make room for me. It was impossible, she wouldn't do such a thing. And with each spin of the pedals a new detail came back to me and suddenly took on all its significance in the light of this sinister revelation.

The keys that she was supposed to have forgotten to take to her colleague.

I pedalled.

Her haste to go and wash as soon as she got home. Had she agreed to one last client? Just to please her madam – she was bound to be attached to her, after all these years. Or for the sake of a regular who was so insistent that she preferred to comply rather than explain? It would be quicker. Bound to be a jealous client, one who was in love. She must have had dozens like that. Perhaps he was the one who had written the letter. To frighten her, to hurt her. To take revenge on her for giving everything up for someone else.

I pedalled. I had to catch up with her.

And that sculpture she'd brought back, out of the blue. The only thing she cared about from her room back there, where she had left all the rest of her past, that 'past that didn't count'. Because the room where she had taken me was not her room: it suddenly made sense.

I pedalled.

The way she turned this way and that as she prepared the chicory, opening all the cupboard doors until she found the cups; and I'd thought it was emotion that had made her hesitant.

And the way she failed to answer when I asked her about the plants she had growing in those pots. She didn't know. Quite simply because that was not her room.

I pedalled. One village after another, but not fast enough.

She must have asked friends to lend her the room, just for the time she needed to take me somewhere.

I pedalled.

The ugly underwear. How horrible to have come in another woman's smell.

I pedalled.

And that strange crucifix above the bed, which I had taken for a sign of piety. I hadn't understood a thing. She wanted to make love with her 'husband', not with a man 'like the others'. It was her way of showing respect for me, in order not to sully me, to give me a more important role in her life; it was the only solution she had found to keep me from becoming part of the dark mass of men who had been bedding her for months, for years.

I pedalled. I was watching out for the forest on the horizon.

Had she recognised someone from that dark mass in the bar where I'd been waiting for her? Was that why she didn't come in and just knocked on the windowpane? And the restaurant where we had dinner: had she chosen it because she was sure she wouldn't see anyone she knew there?

I pedalled furiously. I had already gone past the signpost for N. and the hairpin bend. The lake was only a few hundred metres away. But as I went past L'Escalier I slowed down, instinctively, as I had done so often on those evenings filled with disappointment. And what if she, too, had stopped there instinctively, what if she had felt her resolve flagging? What if her feelings for Louise had once again prevailed, offering her reassurance? Whispering that a child loves its mother no matter who or what she is or has been. I hunted for her bicycle, it might be somewhere, leaning against a wall. But there was no sign of life, other than a curtain fluttering as it was sucked in through the French doors in a room on the ground floor. Like a ghost. The vision made me pedal that much faster: I had to get there in time, I had to stop her.

Had she coughed last night on purpose? Merely pretending to have an asthma attack? Preferring to be taken by the Germans than by me? We weren't risking anything, it had already happened to friends of hers and they'd been released…That way she'd be granted a night's reprieve and she wouldn't be faced with the difficult task of refusing me, wouldn't be obliged to make excuses. We would make love as husband and wife or not at all.

She was so happy this morning. She was going to start all over, rebuild her life, rebuild everything with Louise and me. She wanted to escape from the life she was leading, and whoever wrote her that letter must have known it and couldn't bear the thought.

I pedalled. With every bend in the road I hoped to see her appear, hoped to catch up with her, hold her in my arms and tell her that I agreed, yes, there is always a part of another person's past which does not matter. Or perhaps I might find her curled up at the edge of the lake, because she lacked the courage, because to be human is to be cowardly, and a good thing too. Or because she had come to her senses and realised that I would not abandon her because of it, that I didn't give a damn. Or perhaps she would have gone no further in the water because this was where, on summer evenings they used to picnic with her parents, the three of them. I'd see her silhouetted against the horizon. I'd see her and put my arms around her. And we would kiss, deeply, sincerely, our first adult kiss that would be nothing like our children's kisses. And nothing we had planned that morning would have changed, we would go to the church and get married in that place where I had first begun to love her. And we would be the first bride and groom to be married without wedding rings, but Father André would make an exception in our case, because he knew we were 'those inseparable kids', and because lovebirds, after all, don't have fingers.

You always hope you will get there in time, before it's too late.

I called out at the top of my lungs. I shouted her name as I ran around the lake, and then I saw her bike in the tall grass by the water's edge. And just there, by the rear tyre, there was a spot that had been cleared of a few stones. I feared she had filled her pockets with them, and now they were at the bottom of the lake with her. I jumped in. I dived in here and there, but the silt made it almost impossible to see. Or was it my tears, I don't know. When I finally gave up, it had been dark for a long time. I waited for Annie's body to rise to the surface. Stones could drown a doll, but not a corpse bloated with water. The force of the water would be stronger than the stones. Paper-scissors-stone. WATER.

Annie's body never rose to the surface.

Annie has always been a part of my life. I was two years old, just a few days short of my second birthday, when she was born; and I was twenty when she died, a few days short of twenty. If when you're a few days short of two you don't realise you're about to meet the love of your life, when you're a few days short of twenty you do know when that love has died. And you wonder why you still exist. There are people who think they will die when their inseparable other disappears, but I have always known that we are not so fortunate; my father never murmured to my mother that one could 'die of love'.

For two weeks there were no more letters.

This man bursts into my life claiming that my mother is not my mother, that my so-called mother – this 'Annie' – was dead, and then he goes and disappears, just like that, never mind that I can no longer sleep at night.

He could have provided a conclusion, could have said: That's it, I think you get the picture, you are Louise. I'm sorry to inform you in this way, but here is my telephone number, call me if you would like to talk about it…

No, that would be asking too much, too complicated for a guy who believes that secrets should die with the people who keep them. So why did he open his filthy trap, the bastard? My mother was dead, right? Both mothers, in fact!

It wasn't my name, after all. It wasn't my date of birth, either. I tried to find comfort where I could. And I still didn't have a clue about this possible village somewhere, beginning with N, where there was supposed to be a timber-frame church. And all the other clues were slipping through my fingers, too.

'There was an art gallery in the street perpendicular to hers, I had to go past it and then take the first right. Number 65.

I rang the bell.

It was Madame M. who opened. She was holding the baby in her arms.'

As far as I could recall, we had never lived at a number 65 anywhere.

'L'Escalier was the name given to a fine estate in the middle of our little village, as out of place as a swan among starlings.'

There, too, I found it hard to believe that my parents would never have mentioned that house to me. And I had done my research, to see if there was a hamlet or a place by the name of L'Escalier – to no avail. I was walking on quicksand.

'And what if my next breath proved to be my last? Terrified, I held my breath and turned to the statue of Saint Roch, imploring him; he had cured the lepers, so surely he could save me.'

Roch [Rok], Saint. Saint born ca. 1300–1350, who cured plague sufferers during a pilgrimage to Rome. When he in turn succumbed, he withdrew

147

in isolation into a forest. An angel cared for him, a local dog brought him bread, and he recovered. He would later die in prison, forsaken by all those who knew him. In the course of the 15th century the faithful began to worship him all over Europe, but this declined with the gradual disappearance of the plague, which the saint was said to guard against. Saint Roch is typically portrayed with a pilgrim's staff in his hand. Sometimes he is also shown carrying a satchel, and the hood and cape of a pilgrim. A dog at his side tugs on his cape to show the wound the saint has on his leg. He is invoked whenever epidemics of contagious disease afflict a city. Many monuments, churches, and chapels have been devoted to him. (*The Petit Robert of Proper Names.*)

Trying to find that particular church with its statue of Saint Roch was like trying to find a needle in a haystack. Just like trying to find the village of 'N.' with its lake. Or the place where *La Gazette* was read: you can't get a name for a newspaper much more common than that.

'Rue de la Sablière. Rue Hippolyte-Maindron. 14. 32. 46. I don't know how I managed to find Alberto's studio. 46, rue Hippolyte-Maindron. Perhaps the puppet strings, once again.'

I went to that address. It was the studio of Alberto Giacometti, no less!
And everything fitted. He did indeed have a brother, Diego, and both of them had fled a few days before the

Germans invaded Paris. But he was dead now, so he couldn't tell me anything. 'Alberto Giacometti' – it was too outlandish to be true. My parents would have told me about him.

This discovery was something of a relief, because I tried to see it as the proof that all those letters were nothing more than a writer's wild imaginings. I felt reassured.

Perhaps he would finally show up at my office. 'Ah-hah! I had you there for a while, didn't I – so, will you publish me?'

And it would all finish over a good lunch. And I would go and visit my mother's grave and tell her the whole story, and apologise for ever having doubted her.

The telephone rang.

The moment I heard the telephone, either here or at the office, I immediately thought it must be Nicolas: would he tell me he was sorry he'd spoken to me like that? That he had thought it over, and that there were plenty of people who didn't expect to have a baby and who managed very well, so why shouldn't we?

'Hello, Professor Winnicott here. Your assistant gave me your telephone number. She said you're doing research into timber-frame churches.'

He was an American academic who had been living in Paris for nearly fifteen years; he still had a thick accent. He had been sent over by an American museum at the time of the business with the church at Nuisement-aux-Bois.

Nuisement-aux-Bois: it started with N. I listened carefully, my ear pressed against the receiver.

It went back a few years. The terrible floods in Paris

between 1910 and 1955 had led to the decision to build several reservoir dams along the Seine and its tributaries in order to control the devastating overflow. But the construction of the Der-Chantecoq lake on the Marne had in turn been the cause of another veritable tragedy: three villages were erased from the surface of the earth from one day to the next. All that remains of Chantecoq is the name it gave to the lake. There was also Champaubert-aux-Bois and Nuisement-aux-Bois. The inhabitants, helpless to prevent it, had watched as the forest was uprooted and cleared, their houses dismantled and burned, and their village razed to the ground and covered with water. So that Paris would no longer be flooded. They were devastated. Evicted from their homes, to see them disappear for the so-called public good: you have to have experienced such a thing to understand what it's like; some people never recover. The Indians died of it.

But as every tragedy has its little miracle, there was one church that was rescued, a church and a cemetery. Nuisement.

'And that is where I come in, Mademoiselle Werner. As this church is typical of the charming timber-frame constructions that are so abundant in the Champagne region, a friend in the United States who is a curator wanted to have it for his museum. He appointed me as his intermediary here. I think we owe the rescue of the church to him. If the United States had not been interested, no doubt it would have sunk to the bottom of the lake like the rest of those three villages. But because this man wanted it, he sparked others to want it, as often happens in life. The church was taken apart and rebuilt piece by piece in a little village just next to the former Nuisement-aux-Bois, Sainte-Marie-du-Lac. All the bodies in the cemetery were also exhumed and reburied in exactly the same places behind the church. The inauguration of this miraculous little survivor was held four years ago now, on 12 September 1971, to be exact. That is all I can tell you about the church at Nuisement, I hope it can be of use.'

'What is your first name, Monsieur Winnicott?'

'Robert. Why do you ask?'

'No particular reason. Thank you for all the information.'

For a split second I thought Louis might be hiding behind this Monsieur Winnicott, but the moment this hypothesis occurred to me I realised it was impossible. Louis used French the way one uses one's native language, not an adopted one.

I called Mélanie to thank her for having unearthed this precious source of information, and I told her I would not be coming to the office the next day, either; I had some personal things to take care of.

I dashed into the shower, dressed warmly, grabbed my car keys and a road map. There was not much left of Nuisement-aux-Bois, but the church and the cemetery might be of some help.

On my way out I bumped into Madame Merleau who was about to ring at my door.

She had a package to give me that would not fit in my letter box, as it was too bulky. Was everything all right?

I hadn't been out for four days, she was beginning to worry. Yes, everything was fine. I didn't have time to pour my heart out, and I practically grabbed the package out of her hands to inspect the handwriting.

Obviously I hadn't heard the last of Louis. I would read it on the way.

From Paris, head towards Vitry-le-François. From Vitry-le-François, take the D13 in the direction of the Lac de Der as far as Troyes. From there take the road for Sainte-Marie-du-Lac.

The envelope contained a package wrapped in brown paper and a very short note, once again in Louis's hand.

Dear Camille,

I thought I knew all there was to know about this story, and it took me years to understand what had really happened. I wasn't expecting anything else, because I always thought I knew the truth. Until I was told at last.

I am not angry with Annie for having hidden it from me: she knew how powerful jealousy can be. She had already paid the price.

I immediately recognised her, not from her appearance, but the moment she opened her mouth. It was like an apparition. Her voice did not have the evenness of dialogue; instead she told me the whole long story in one go. With all the immodesty of a guilty woman. And with no thought for my feelings. I felt I had no right to interrupt her. Everything was crystal clear; filthy, but crystal clear.

*

Dear Camille

With those two words my heart was in my mouth.

Oddly, it was at that moment that I knew I was Louise.

I unwrapped the brown paper. Inside was a school exercise book. I opened it.

Louis' handwriting, as always, more cramped and more vigorous, but this time, writing someone else's words.

*

Everything I have done was in order not lose my husband. I'm not looking for any excuses, I don't have any. All I know is that I loved that man more than anything on earth.

I don't really know where to begin.

The first thing that comes to mind is the argument we had at L'Escalier.

The sound of his typewriter woke me at dawn. My husband was a journalist. He worked a great deal, and having to go back and forth between L'Escalier and his office in Paris did not make his days any shorter. I was often asleep when he came home, but every morning I brought him a cup of coffee which he drank with me. That morning, he spilled it.

'I cannot believe it, at least a hundred people have died, there've been over thirty thousand arrests, everyone's talking about it, and this comes as news to you?'

Yes, it was news to me. In Germany Goebbels was baying for blood as he hunted down the Jews, and

*

*

those Nazi scum had broken so many shop windows and ransacked homes that they called it Kristallnacht... The more my husband explained what had happened, the more I felt his anger towards me. Suddenly, it overflowed.

'This cannot go on! If I agreed to move here, it was so you would feel better, not so you would go on feeling sorry for yourself. I do not recognise you. You don't give a damn about anything, except whether I bought your canvas, your charcoal, your paint...It is not by shutting yourself off from the rest of the world that you are going to solve your problem. And now you've made me late!'

'You do that! Get out! Go back to your wonderful world where everybody knows about everything...Go and tell your dear readers how the world works and above all don't waste your time explaining it to me, how our world is going to work with everything that's happening to us.'

This was the first argument we'd ever had; as if I could hear the cry for blood here too, I could tell something bad was coming. It was 11 November 1938.

My husband was right, I hadn't been reading the papers for weeks. I couldn't stand the campaign that was raging for an increased birth rate; wherever you looked, the same injunction:

'Have more children! Have more children, France must make up for her losses in 1914'

'60 million in France will be a guarantee of peace!'

*

156

*

So what? Four deaths for zero births, it was not my fault if I could not improve the ratio in our family.

For nearly six years now Paul and I had been trying to have a child.

We were married on 16 March 1932. I was nineteen, Paul was twenty. By sealing our union, the church bells also began the countdown to conception: in our milieu marriage and children were inseparable.

In the beginning all the mothers in my circle would share their experiences with me; those who were pregnant were the most unbearable, for they thought they were the purveyors of holy writ. Such female solidarity with regard to pregnancy seems to be in the nature of things, like shared male laughter when a lewd joke is told.

In the beginning, they all tried to be reassuring. I had to wait until nature was ready. They were sure it was only a question of months. And then came our parents' sudden death; we must not underestimate the shock of it.

That was true, we must not underestimate the shock...

The telephone had rung during the night, our wedding night. Our parents' car had gone off the road, on their way home. It wasn't a dangerous bend. The driver was drunk. All four of them were killed.

Neither Paul nor I ever wanted to know whose father was behind the wheel. We were much too afraid that

*

we would reproach one another for it, sooner or later, in the course of an argument or a moment of resentment. We already reproached ourselves for not having taken the time to say goodbye to them that night, eager as we were to be alone at last.

And after that, we were alone all right. It was a horrible, relentless time. I cannot even remember how many nights, early in our marriage, ended in tears.

After our shared tears we tried to hide our sorrow, to keep each other from feeling worse. We lived like that for weeks, two red-eyed individuals who would suddenly rush out of the room to go and hide in a place where we could weep alone.

We came to terms with our strange, sad family situation as best we could. It was like a void and a burden at the same time, like a long endless fall that would stop only with a pregnancy, or at least that is what I hoped. I prayed that an infant's cries would put an end to this macabre silence. Moreover, it would be a way of seeing them again, somehow: in a nose, a mouth, the shape of a face. Our beloved parents.

Like all those who truly love one another, we enjoyed our time alone together. But the tragedy for us was that, from now on, that is all there would ever be. And yet our family reunions had been so joyful. Our parents had got along marvellously, and we used to seize every opportunity to dine together. They even saw one another without us. When he saw the wedding cake, my father, with his usual sense of humour, could not help but quip, 'It is not an arranged marriage we are celebrating this evening but an arranged friendship!' And he had raised his champagne glass in a toast to

Paul's parents. 'Champagne!' I often wondered if that sip was one of those that had killed them.

It was like a punishment in a Greek tragedy. Death resembling a curse. So when we were unable to conceive, it was as if fate was trying all the harder to hound us. Was our lineage doomed to vanish from the planet? Was this God's will?

Three years went by: nothing. All my friends had children. Some were already expecting their second child, whereas I was still sporting a 'svelte figure'. Inquisitive gazes had become pitying. It was no longer the problem of when; the problem was now me: they were absolutely sure of that. Muttered conversations had replaced advice; we had gone from the things others speak about without giving you the right to speak, to the things one simply does not speak about.

I felt so helpless, so alone. Neither Paul nor I ever broached the subject, either. I had no one to confide in.

Pasquin, our family doctor, was a charming man, but he could not help sharing the problems of his consulting table with his dinner table.

'This sole is delicious! It is excellent for your health, did you know that, ladies? A woman who eats fish will increase her fertility tenfold. Oh, and now that I think of it, I must tell poor Madame Werner, it might help her…'

And that is how two mouthfuls of sole and the patter worthy of a fairground hawker was enough to prove that I was infertile.

Books were all that was left. I had to find help somewhere. I was so ashamed that I went into a bookshop on the Left Bank, far from home, and I even pretended the books were for a friend.

✳

The expert in the matter was a certain Auguste Debay.

Health and physiology of marriage. A natural and medical history of married men and women. Health and hygiene for pregnant women and infants.

If I remember such a complicated title so accurately, it must be because I found myself imagining that the book had cured the infertility of the bookseller's wife. I clung to any hope I could find. To be sure, this Debay book dated from 1885, but it was still the leading reference book. There was not a single contemporary book on the subject.

'Have more children! Have more children, France must make up for her losses in 1914'

The government did not pull any punches to increase the birth rate: abortion was prohibited, contraception as well, and while they were at it, so was any information whatsoever to do with sexuality. Already the fact that no one talked about it meant that things weren't about to get any better. Their strategy was straightforward: the less people knew about it, the freer nature would be to do her work. They could have tried to combat infertility, it would have meant a few more births, but power knows how to prohibit, not how to cure. And in those days, infertile women were just a handful of inconvenient second class citizens whom they preferred to ignore. Their calculations were precise: the loss of thirty grams of sperm was the equivalent of one thousand two hundred grams of blood. Waste must be avoided, and all the medical tomes denounced

*

copulation with infertile women and their 'destructive, useless lovemaking'.

This bookseller was obviously very well informed on the matter. As I worked my way along the shelves of his shop, I was seized by a mad hope. In a few seconds I would be holding *the* 'reference book' in my hands, and while it might be dated, it still remained *the* reference book. And after all, if old wives' remedies worked, I could just as easily go for advice to the doctors who looked after those old wives.

The bookseller handed me the volume, quietly wishing me good luck. He must be used to catering to women like me who came to look for books they maintained were not for their own use. He must recognise them by the way they snatched up the books and held them against their chest, the way one might hold a remedy, not a printed text.

The man's discretion touched me, and I thanked him sincerely. It was vital to me not to lie to the one person who had held his hand out to me in so many months. This might be a sinister thought, but I realise that that bookseller was the last individual in my life to whom I did not lie.

Health and physiology of marriage. A natural and medical history of married men and women. Health and hygiene for pregnant women and infants.

I threw myself into the book heart and soul, and believe me, that is more than just a mere expression.

If one were to believe what one read, having children was not difficult, it was merely a question of one's health. Already trapped in a mindless spiral of desperate hope, I followed all the advice.

*

To fight against the 'inertia of genital organs' one must favour 'stimulating nutrition'. My maid Sophie served nothing but the so-called recommended food: rocket, celery, artichokes, asparagus, truffles…I wolfed everything down when my husband wasn't looking, then forced myself to dine with him as well, even though I was no longer hungry. The very thought of sitting down to a meal became a nightmare. But I took comfort in the knowledge that so many infertile women had become fertile.

> 1 litre of Malaga wine
> 30 grams of vanilla pod
> 30 grams of cinnamon
> 30 grams of ginseng
> 30 grams of rhubarb
> Allow to macerate for two weeks.

I drank this supposedly aphrodisiac wine, and turned everything I knew – jam, syrup – into an aphrodisiac concoction. It was pathetic. I even took aphrodisiac baths. Rosemary, sage, oregano, mint, and camomile blossoms. Five hundred grams of each, which I let infuse for twelve hours then poured into my bath. Over time my skin acquired a spicy scent that disgusted me.

And then I began to take medication which I prepared myself, but always on the basis of the ingredients listed in Debay's book. Pills. Liniments. Plasters. My bathroom had become a regular dispensary. Every act, every gesture was orchestrated with a view to conceiving, but time was passing, and nothing worked.

My agitation made me forfeit all sense of moderation,

∗

*

and the escalation in treatments turned horribly wrong. After all, Anne of Austria had managed to give birth to Louis XIV after twenty-three years of infertility. Ablutions in burning hot water just before intercourse. Flagellation of the loins, thighs and buttocks with a birch switch. And the most unbearable of all, urtication: I had to rub my genitals with the fruit of the wild rose, which caused the most terrible itching.

It may sound unsavoury, but it is the truth. I had become my own guinea pig and the only thing that would have stopped me was pregnancy. At that time, advice of this nature was the only remedy available for those who wanted a child when the body itself refused to comply with the wishes of one's soul. Theories only become archaic the moment new ones replace them, and for almost sixty years nothing at all had been written about infertile women.

Then there was my husband's grandmother's birthday.

At the end of the lunch, Granny tapped her spoon against her saucer to get everyone's attention; she wanted to thank all of us – sixteen of us – for having come. Everyone applauded. Then suddenly a voice cried out, 'There aren't sixteen of us, Grandmother, only fifteen!'

With a twinkle in her eye, the old woman counted again and shook her head.

'I'm not senile yet, when I say "sixteen" I have my own way of calculating!'

Just then, someone understood what she meant. Cries of enthusiasm, then the names of all the women sitting around the table: 'Marine!' 'Catherine!' 'Mathilde!' 'Bérengère?' 'Emma!' 'Virginie?'

*

*

Every name except Granny's and my own. Because it was no longer possible for her; and because for me, it never had been. Paul squeezed my hand under the table. The guests preferred the spontaneity of a guessing game over the idea of observing the feelings of others or, above all, tact. Finally, quietly, like a musical instrument that has been tuned at last, the names receded until there was only one left: 'Mathilde! Mathilde!' And to be sure, the heroine of the day was beaming with pleasure, as she should, under the circumstances. Everyone applauded. And amidst the applause, the heroine of the day spoke solemnly about the child she was carrying: her voice was earnest and somewhat flat, no doubt because she already had all she could wish for.

Suddenly her eyes met mine and she looked away at once, her broad radiant smile frozen on her face, and a moment of awkwardness spread round the table. Silence. The game had yielded to the weight of reality, my reality. At that moment I realised I had become 'the infertile woman' in the family, the one whose presence absolutely precluded any displays of joy, the one who was so unfortunate that the happiness of others could prove fatal. My shame was confirmed.

My infertility had taken over my whole life. I could no longer have a conversation. My anger or sadness about any subject at all was never taken at face value. I could see what everyone was thinking: she is angry because she cannot have a child, she is sad because she cannot have a child. My opinion as such no longer mattered.

They must all have thought that it was shame that led to my hasty departure, and they were right. But

*

164

they would never admit that they were the ones who brought the shame down upon me.

I will acknowledge that Paul did everything in his power to ensure our departure went smoothly. He never complained about the numerous trips he had to make between Nuisement and Paris, either for his work or to attend a dinner. Because he could still join in that life; men have no such concerns amongst themselves.

I did not want there to be any reminders of my infertility at L'Escalier, and everyone seemed to have concurred to make this easy for me. No one came to visit, and it was not difficult to cut myself off, all that was required was to leave Paris behind. As for the others, Paul did his utmost to avoid the subject; Sophie excelled at her job by pretending not to know, although she knew perfectly well and Jacques, my husband's handyman, was only interested in such matters insofar as they applied to animals.

Even with Alberto I was fortunate…He was one of those people whose discretion meant he would only refer to a problem if he had a solution to offer. Alberto Giacometti was one of my friends, and he had agreed to give painting lessons to Annie.

Annie was just Annie, a local girl. And above all, the only person threatening my fragile equilibrium.

She often painted in the vicinity of L'Escalier and I could see her off in the distance. One day I asked Jacques to invite her in for tea, I felt in need of company. She got into the habit of coming to the house to work, and of course I went along with it. Contrary to all expectations, I appreciated the young girl's presence, enjoying it rather than merely enduring it. She was the

✳

first person in so long who did not view me as a failed mother. If she needed something for her painting, I was only too happy to send for it. It was as if I had at last found someone on whom I could happily lavish my frustrated maternal instinct. I would not go so far as to say she came to replace the child I could not have, that would be too much of a caricature, but there was something of that in my relationship with her, and caricature can be a part of life.

She never asked about it. She was not surprised to find out that my husband and I had no children, and I knew by this that she was making neither a statement nor a criticism. It simply did not occur to her. As she was not a prisoner of convention, Annie did not find me abnormal.

It was November 1938.

I was convinced that the best way to control my misfortune was to keep it to myself. I avoided speaking to her about it. I would rather she knew nothing about it and above all I was surprised to find that when I was in her company I could forget about it.

Unfortunately one cannot spend one's life avoiding such a topic. Neither between a man and a woman who love one another, nor between two women whose friendship is sincere.

One day I told her everything. Down to the last detail. I could not stop talking, like an alcoholic who needs to pour out words, any words at all, to anyone at all. She was the first person in whom I could confide, and it was disturbing, enlightening, even, to hear myself giving voice to my emotions, but I immediately regretted it. I had ruined everything, and I knew it.

*

*

She was sitting opposite me, crushed by my unhappiness, unsure how to react. And I immediately recognised the shame I had wanted to cast off by leaving Paris. The same shame that clung to me and made me suddenly lower my head and place both hands beneath my chin. It was that intense weariness, which I had managed to shrug off in Annie's presence. I had ruined everything. I wept over my own cowardice.

To confide in someone is a sign of love or friendship, and it must be handled with extreme tact. Not everyone can listen to another's secrets, and a child even less so. A person's character must be shaped before one burdens it with things it is not yet equipped to understand. Adults who confide in children disgust me. I disgust myself. But that day I was not adult enough myself to realise just how young Annie was. Too young for me to confide in, too young to respond with advice. As she could not fulfil the traditional role of a confidant, she had no other choice than to allow herself to be profoundly affected by my despair. But as is often the case when one person opens her heart, the other follows suit.

Annie did not want children. She was categorical about it, astonishingly resolute on the topic for her age. I saw how intensely her eyes shone, how delicately her hands folded her table napkin. That was typical Annie, in that moment: extremely assured, extremely gentle. I think her charm derived in part from that strange combination. Thrilling and soothing. She saw life as something more than just filled with children. Now I understood better why, when I was with her, my infertility had seemed so easy to bear.

'It's not compatible with motherhood,' she added,

*

before reciting a long list of women who had to give up painting once they became mothers. A friend of hers had told her this, a young man she was very fond of. A certain Louis.

She also talked to me about her parents, who had waited for her until they reached that ultimate threshold where one no longer expects to fall pregnant. But immediately upon the joy of her birth came the fear of losing her. Her mother surrounded her with endless precautions, and worried about everything. Her father tried to reason with his wife, and they always ended up quarrelling. In the evening, her mother often slipped into her bed. Annie suspected she deliberately instigated these quarrels in order to be able to sleep next to her daughter, to hear her breathing and know that everything was fine, that her little girl was well and truly alive. Unintentionally, she had conveyed to Annie that having children was a heavy responsibility, a source of imminent tragedy.

Annie was laconic and sensitive, and that's why I liked her; she did not talk like others her age or from her background.

All the same, she was still young, the age where one does not yet know that for certain problems there are no solutions. And she wanted to find one, any solution at all. She should never have gone ahead with it.

She offered to have a child instead of me.

Forgive me, I'm expressing myself poorly. To have a child for me.

It was 7 February 1939. I was still sitting with my head down on my hands beneath my chin, my gaze riveted on the newspaper next to my plate, staring at

*

the date the way a body grabs at anything to keep from falling.

At the time, I swear, her proposal had seemed completely ridiculous, thoughtless, naïve. But despair is a sly evil, it gathers strength at night, and that very evening I began to reconsider her proposal. What if that were the real reason we had met? Was it God's will?

In those days I was constantly putting myself in God's hands, a habit that had arisen out of distress. I was neither devout nor a regular churchgoer, but I was simply and foolishly superstitious, that was all I was capable of. Superstition, unlike faith, is for those who need to believe but cannot give, like myself at the time, enclosed in the selfishness of misfortune.

The day I had decided to leave Paris I had felt so devastated that I was incapable of making more than one decision at a time. When I opened the drawer of my husband's desk, the one where he kept the keys to our properties, I had shuffled through the keys frenetically, before grabbing one without looking at it. It was the key to L'Escalier. I didn't question my choice, but attributed it to God.

Had He thus intended for me to meet this girl who would enable me to return to Paris with a child in my arms? In this business God will have served, in the end, to make me commit the most dreadful deeds.

One day I caught myself gazing at Annie's belly, and I imagined it growing round with my child.

With this first glimmer of hope I understood the true source of my anxiety, one I had never dared formulate for fear it might transpire: that Paul would leave me.

Our milieu required the presence of a child, but

✳

did he? What did he think when he looked at all the women he encountered? Did he occasionally find them attractive, not only because they were beautiful, but also because they might be able to provide him with a child?

Paul, my husband, my love: this misfortune got the better of us. But we were so much in love with each other. Before.

I knew by heart the ideal conditions for conception. Before resorting to other methods I had begun with them myself, and I was determined to apply them to Annie and my husband.

The act itself must not last longer than three minutes; all the doctors agreed that pleasure would compromise the chances for conception. What were three minutes in exchange for a child. And I was convinced that once would be enough for God to provide me with this relief, just once. I know, that was stupid of me, but 'errors often arise from certainty', as Paul was in the habit of saying.

'Didn't I tell you that his Munich agreement was utter rubbish – how on earth could they think that Hitler would stop there? Too often errors arise from certainty. First it was the Rhineland, then the Anschluss, and now the Sudetenland. This new deal will hardly suffice to put a stop to that madman's demands. Next time it will be war, I assure you.'

That was on 16 March 1939. Paul and I were walking through the grounds at L'Escalier. Hitler had invaded Prague, and Czechoslovakia was finished. Paul was convinced that war was unavoidable. I didn't want to believe it so I gently poked fun at his pessimism. I

*

was so obsessed by Annie's proposal that I could think of nothing else. The air was mild, it was our wedding anniversary, and I told myself this would be the best time to talk to him about it.

'How can you ask me to do such a thing?…Have you taken leave of your senses? She's only a kid, she doesn't know what she's talking about. She said the first thing that came into her mind. What are you thinking? First you want to move, and you don't seem to care in the least if it harms my career. And now I am supposed to sleep with the first girl who comes along? What next? Will I have to kidnap a child after I've killed its parents? You're going mad. I beg you, get a hold of yourself. Let me take you in my arms, darling – you got pregnant once, you'll get pregnant again, I promise you.'

But I did not let him take me into his arms, and moreover, after that day we were never much in each other's arms any more. I walked as far as the birthwort arbour and sat down. Paul was standing there in front of me. He was nervously trying to adjust a branch around the metal arch. I tried to speak as clearly as possible.

'I never was pregnant. Pasquin lied to you.'

That had been two years earlier. One day I missed my period, and it did not come in the days that followed. All during those endless months of waiting I had imagined a thousand ways to tell Paul that I was pregnant; I had never been able to use any of them.

He held me in his arms with so much love: he had been so afraid that we might never have a child, he was so proud, he promised me he would be the best father I could dream of. We spent the night making a thousand plans – we who had stopped making plans at all. The

*

*

next afternoon I had an appointment with Dr Pasquin for an examination, and I stopped by the market on the way. We had invited our closest friends to dinner, so eager were we to share our happiness with them.

I never found out how the meal went, nor how Paul shared our good news with them. When I came back from the appointment, I apologised that I was not feeling well and went straight up to bed. I let them celebrate an event that would never happen. I didn't have the heart to tell Paul the truth.

I wasn't pregnant. Pasquin was sorry, I was simply suffering from amenorrhea, which was not a serious condition. Not serious? How could he say such a thing?

I did not leave my bed all week. Paul thought it was my pregnancy that had made me tired, and he was the soul of thoughtfulness. Every morning he read all the letters of congratulations that people sent to us. I stopped eating. Worried, he called Pasquin to my bedside.

When the door closed behind them, I felt a terrible sense of relief. Pasquin would tell him everything: a minor case of amenorrhea et cetera. But when the door opened again, Paul gave me a sweet smile and as he pulled the covers up over me, he murmured that it was not so bad, if I had got pregnant once I would get pregnant again, I mustn't worry, we would manage, he loved me.

Although I wept and told Paul I had never been pregnant, that I was infertile – it was all in vain. He ran his hand over my forehead and told me to be calm, it was normal for me to be delirious after what I had just been through, the doctor had warned him. I stopped

*

my crying, Paul would not believe me, he did not wa
to believe me. Pasquin told him I was suffering fro
depression, that it happened to many women after
miscarriage. When for once he should have told th
truth, Pasquin had kept my secret.

'A few days before the time of the month when
the period is due, apply six small leeches to the
vulva, that is, three to the inside of each of the
labia minora. As soon as the leeches drop off,
press a small wad of agaric mushroom to the
bites in order to stem the flow of blood and stop
it completely. Finally, twice a day for three days,
inject stimulating solutions into the vagina, with:

Liquid ammonia...4 gr
Chilled mixture of brewed nettle..............250 gr

'It is rare that the menstrual cycle fails to be re-
established after this treatment.

'Many women, especially young girls, find the
application of leeches repugnant; they may, before
resorting to this extreme measure, try to have a
sitz bath with the water at 30 degrees, some strong
rubbing at the orifice of the vulva, mustard baths
for the feet, cupping glasses on the inner thighs
and a few stimulating purgatives and enema
finally, suffuse the vagina with steam fro
boiling water and expose the open part to a go
fire in order to stimulate it. Through these vari
means, an absent period may be restored; if
not, one must resort to the previous measure

Paul was tearing the birthwort leaves to shreds. He was pale. Despite the fact that he was looking down, I could see his eyes blinking rapidly, which with him is a sign of extreme nervousness. I had just destroyed a reality he would never have been capable of imagining, quite simply because he did not suspect the existence of a quarter of the elements that composed it.

He nodded his head at last, his eyes staring at a point in front of him, and I knew he was about to say something.

'If I asked you to make love with another man in order to have a child, you would accept, is that what you are trying to say? You think I'm not making enough of an effort? Then so be it…If to be a husband worthy of the name you think I have to sleep with that girl, then I shall do it. Because I love you, do you hear me? Only because I love you. But only once, no more, because after that you will have to get this madness out of your head and let us never speak of it again.'

It is strange how we are made. No sooner had Paul understood that the energy I had deployed in trying to convince him had now turned to despair, than he capitulated. Three minutes in exchange for a child: suddenly the equation no longer seemed so simple.

I was not jealous by nature, and no one, neither my husband nor Annie, could have foreseen that this moody disposition would erupt in love. Nor did I for that matter; I had not yet reached the age where one is no longer fooled by one's own nature.

Even today I wonder whether I actually made that

proposal to him so that he would reject it. Simply to initiate the conversation between us. So that he would reassure me and tell me he would never leave me, that I would not be repudiated the way other women had been. Catherine of Aragon, Joséphine de Beauharnais, Princess Soraya…I would not be the first woman to have been abandoned because of her infertility. Not to mention all the ones we don't know about.

But perhaps if he had refused I would have been angry with him, too. In fact, the answer to the question I had asked was bound to be unacceptable.

If he had said no, I would think he didn't love me.

He had said yes, and I still thought he didn't love me.

Suddenly all the indecency of the situation became painfully obvious. So I wrote him a letter where I told him everything he had to do. I still see myself working out the constraints to make the act as impersonal as possible. According to all the doctors, the missionary position was the only reasonable form of copulation, and the union must take place in a bed and nowhere else, the bed being 'the only altar where the work of the flesh can be accomplished with dignity', I still remember these words, 'in utter silence and darkness'. The doctors also proscribed the presence of any mirrors in the conjugal bedchamber, 'abject objects promoting a loss of concentration'. I could feel my jealousy, how damp my fingers had become around my pen. Those three minutes already seemed to me like an eternity. My torture.

During the night, with Jacques' help, I made the room without walls into a suitable venue, and the next day Annie was treated to the same lecture as my

*

husband. But in her case, in person. My persistent bad faith allowed me to reason that I too would have liked someone to explain to me in infinite detail what to expect from my first sexual encounter.

In fact, my explanations were not meant to reassure her, far from it: I wanted to frighten her, to incite her to refuse so that she would stop this time bomb for me. I was certain that the sight of her studio transformed into a brothel would upset her, I thought that I would be able to reach her innermost feelings through the décor if I could not reach them through my words. 'My husband will be back within the hour…' I hoped by pressuring her to make her withdraw.

'Let's wait until tomorrow…'

There, she'd said it. I was sure I had won, that Annie had changed her mind. That she was abandoning the whole idea. I was deeply grateful to her, she was the only one of the three of us who had the pride and the courage to put a halt to this insane scheme.

When she came the next day I had not been expecting her. I spent the following hours hoping that Paul would not come home early. He did come home early. And this improbable scene unfolded before my eyes.

He came into the drawing room. I looked at him. He did not return my gaze. Annie had her head down. He said to her, 'Let's go.' She stood up. Followed him. And I did nothing to stop them. I heard the door to the room without walls close behind them.

I stayed there where they had left me. My pounding heart made my chest rock back and forth imperceptibly; I had trouble catching my breath. Paul would come back, apologetic, and tell me he could not make love to another woman. If someone had slapped me while I waited I would not have felt a thing, I was no longer there. I was in that part of the soul that is unacquainted with the body, perhaps that part of us that survives after death.

Paul was the first to return to the drawing room, and he stood by the fireplace as if a fire were crackling there. That was his place, summer and winter alike. Sleeping with another woman has not deterred him from his habits, I thought. I believe it was in that very moment that I felt truly betrayed: that he should remain standing there by the fireplace. I looked at him. He did not return my gaze.

I hated him for standing there, but at the same time it gave me strength, to have him there before my eyes. I felt a surge of pride. I had to behave as if everything that had just happened was in accordance with my wishes. As if I had no problem signing the contract that I myself had drawn up. And while the effect on me was that of a dead man touching his last will and testament, I managed to go deep inside myself and recover my voice, to call out to Annie as she left the house, 'Goodbye, see you tomorrow.'

She replied with a faraway, 'See you tomorrow.'

Only Paul said nothing. His eyes downcast, staring into the fireplace, he held his hands out as if he wanted to warm them by the fire. It was 9 April. The andirons were empty. Outside the sun was warm. I should have suspected something.

During the month that followed life went on as usual. Annie continued to come to the house, my husband left late morning and came home for dinner, occasionally afterwards, but rarely.

I was the only one who had changed. I no longer hoped for a child the way I had all the previous years; I was expecting it. Serenely. I thought of all the things we would do with our child. Return to Paris, pick up the threads of our former life. I would abandon the pariah status I had been relegated to; nothing more would ever separate Paul and me, we would go to our bed without that heavy burden weighing upon our bodies. We would have a child and expect no others, we would make love the way we had a few years ago, with a lightness of touch. Strengthened by these convictions I was no longer even angry at Paul for having yielded to my entreaties. My jealousy had retreated in the face of such a bright future, and my faith had no bounds.

But on 9 May Paul bluntly informed me that Annie was not pregnant. The news was all the more distressing in that I had not been expecting to hear it from him. This could not be. He must have made a mistake. And why did he know before I did?

'Annie herself told me.'

When? They had not seen each other since.

'Well, no, she didn't tell me. Well, not exactly…We had agreed that if Annie was not pregnant she would wedge the curtain of the room in the window. That way, in the evening, when I came down the drive, I would see the curtain hanging outside and then I would know and could tell you. We decided together, after we… well, you know…once we had finished…'

This was dreadful. That my husband and Annie could have been so complicitous. And yet their fucking had served no purpose. I was mad with despair. I had

*

178

never been in such a state, even for my own sake. This pregnancy was our last chance for salvation. I had resigned myself to the fact that once their two bodies had connected, it would be once and for all. Now they had to try again. They could not give up, not now, they had to go on, until it worked.

Paul stood up straight and refused vehemently: we had made our pact, I had defined the rules – 'just once' – and he had respected them, it was my turn now. We spent all that evening and night arguing. He accused me of wanting to destroy us. I replied that we would be destroyed all the more surely if we failed to have a child.

The next morning he insisted on staying until Annie arrived.

'I don't know what you will go putting into the girl's head this time.'

He was watching for her from the window in the drawing room. The front door had not even opened yet and he was already in the hall. He rushed to meet her and I could hear them from where I sat.

'I told Elisabeth you aren't pregnant, I told her about the curtain, that you wedged it in the window to let me know.'

They came into the drawing room. He was pale, insistent. He was waving in my direction.

'She won't listen. She wants us to go on. I can't get her to see reason, you tell her, tell her it's impossible!'

Annie was giving him a strange look.

'I agree.'

Neither Paul nor I understood at first what she meant.

*

'I agree to go on trying until we manage it.'

Annie said this in the most poised tone imaginable.
My husband stepped away from her, as if she had just
burned him. He seemed completely lost. He hunted
for his briefcase on the mantelpiece, then remembered
he had left it against the wall below the window. He
marched over to it, snatched it up and left the room.

It was as if we were in a play by Feydeau and, in
spite of the palpable tension, Annie and I smiled at his
ridiculous exit. But for the rest there was nothing to
be said, and Annie defused it with her usual natural
good grace, handing me a magazine and saying kindly,
'Come and read next to me, I'd like to get working on
a canvas again.' We could resume our harmonious
coexistence.

Paul and I, on the other hand, no longer spoke. We
ate in silence. Even Sophie no longer dared say a thing.
Normally she would comment on the dishes she served
us – what a good idea it had been to leave the skin of
the aubergine on, for more taste; how lucky we were
to have this good chicken, which would have ended
up in Mrs So-and-So's shopping bag if Sophie hadn't
hurried to be first in the queue...She was a cheerful
sort, Sophie, but the pervading bad mood had got the
better of her chatter.

I was literally possessed by my obsession and, as
with all obsessions, this one was destroying everything
in its wake. Paul had to make this child, by whatever
means possible, and I ended up making the worst
decision of my life, that of refusing to share my bed with
him. I wanted to coerce him somehow into sleeping
with Annie, and while his mind might baulk, his body

✳

would comply. I had driven him into a corner with all the sadism of an enemy, I had forgotten that I loved him.

We could have stayed like that for a long time, entrenched in our positions, surly with one another, but as is often the case in hopeless dilemmas, an outside event suddenly got things moving.

That day Paul came home late morning. It was a Saturday and I was at my dressing table, getting ready. He seemed relieved to find me there. He was extremely agitated, fiddling with all the perfume bottles, and he could not stand still.

'I went to Weidman's execution this morning and the most dreadful thing happened. First of all, the execution was almost an hour late, we still don't know why, but it was broad daylight by the time they bound Weidman and shoved him forward. The photographers were going mad with excitement at the prospect of at last being able to get some good shots of an execution, since up to now they had only got mediocre night-time shots. I could hear their cameras clicking away. The crowd was shouting. Impassive as always, Desfourneaux released the blade. Suddenly a group of women, a horde of hyenas, made their way past the guards and flung themselves on the ground to soak their handkerchiefs in the pools of blood. Weidman's head probably hadn't even stopped rolling at the bottom of the basket.

'It was revolting, those squatting, screaming women, sponging up the blood with their hands. I could not understand what they were doing. It was Eugène who explained it to me. He'd been in a foul temper ever since the trial began. For one thing, he has the same first name as Weidman, and he could no longer go anywhere in the office without some clever idiot slamming his hand against his neck as if to sever his throat, "clack". "Look at those women, they're mad, they think that a lunatic's blood will make them fertile." When he said that, you cannot imagine how afraid I was. I closed my eyes and did not dare open them again. I was afraid you might emerge from the crowd too and kneel down among those women. I stayed on after all the others had left, checking every street corner; it would have been just like you to go there once no one could see you, to kneel down just long enough to take something out of your bag, just long enough to let the hem of your skirt inconspicuously touch the ground, in the hope of absorbing a few drops of blood for you, too. You could have done that, couldn't you? I asked Eugène to write up the story in my place and I hurried home, I wanted to be with you as soon as possible. I am so distraught about everything that is happening to us, my love, I don't want you ever to go somewhere just to let your skirt hem touch the ground, do you hear me? Ever. Do you still want me to go ahead with it?'

'Yes.'

'Is she here?'

'Yes.'

It was 17 June. Eugène Weidman, 'the killer from La Voulzie', six-time assassin, had just been beheaded. And so had I.

*

After that Saturday they got into the habit of meeting every Saturday. It was a secret we shared, but we never spoke about it together – those are the most terrifying kinds of secrets. I had decided I would stay away from the house on those days, and I had Sophie and Jacques leave as well. He would drive us up to Paris, and she would do the shopping: that way they would not suspect what was going on in the room without walls.

Jacques waited for me outside the Normandie. I hoped that going to the cinema would get my mind off things. To be far away and distracted would make things easier than if I stayed in the next room. But one cannot suppress one's thoughts that easily. *You Can't Take It With You*: I remember, it won the Oscar for the best film, people spoke of it very highly, 'a sentimental film by Capra', what harm could there be…Except that sentiment is exasperating when you are caught up in your own drama, and I learned that at my own expense. That day the knot around my soul was pulled too tight for me to digest the film, and while all was well that ended well, to the tune of Polly Wolly Doodle, I burst into tears. Unlike the spectators around me I could find neither happiness nor relief; on the contrary, nothing but misery, rage, dismay. The man I loved was making love to another woman. Instead of removing me to a safe distance from my own drama, the film made it more blatant than ever.

I absolutely had to find a way to get closer to Paul, that much I knew. To give him something in exchange for those Saturdays, to show him how grateful I was to him.

Although I was the one who had turned down all the invitations we'd received since we moved to L'Escalier, now I offered to go with him to the reception at the Polish Embassy and to Sacha Guitry's wedding, both of

*

which I knew he planned to attend, the first for political reasons, and the second for the sake of their friendship. And could we stay and sleep at the house between the two events?

Fine.

At our house in Paris, I mean.

Yes, yes, he knew what I meant.

It was 28 June 1939.

The party at the embassy was lively, but troubling. Everyone who was anyone in Paris was there, utterly carefree, as if the tension between Poland and Germany simply did not exist. Lukasiewicz, the ambassador, danced all evening, barefoot and gesticulating, inviting all and sundry to join him. Even the valets in their livery were dancing, even I was dancing. I had not had so much fun in a long time. A mazurka, a polonaise, a polka...

Paul was aghast. When you thought of the danger they were in, back in Poland...Had they not learned their lesson with Czechoslovakia? Someone next to us retorted in an offhand manner that Lukasiewicz was convinced Hitler was bluffing, that he had it on authority that the Führer had promised the Duce peace until 1943. Paul called him an idiot, but his words were lost in the music.

When the firework display began I reached for his hand. He let me take it, hardly seeming to realise that it had been months since I had shown any gestures of affection. I could tell at that moment how worried he was by the political situation. As for me, light years from any geopolitical considerations, with Paul's hand in mine I was thinking that our baby might be on its way. Look at

*

those magnificent blue fireworks! It would be a boy.

It was 4 July.

I did not sleep well that night, Paul did not come to sleep in my bed, whereas I had imagined I would fall asleep in his arms. He spent the night in his study cleaning his 'collection of collectable pistols' as he called it.

At breakfast he remarked, wasn't life strange, after all: there were some items in his collection he had not seen in such a long time that he found quite charming, while others had lost any charm at all.

I remember his words well, and I know why. It was one of those statements that conceal what they actually mean, and leave an aftertaste with those who say them as well as with those who hear them. A 'key statement' one will remember at a later time as one thinks, So that's what was meant. How could I have failed to realise at the time?

The collection had belonged to his father, and Paul had inherited it upon his death.

He always carried the 'little Derringer' on him. Like a ring that passes from finger to finger among the women in a family, that pistol had been passing for generations from pocket to pocket of the men in my husband's family. They said it was the same model that had been used to assassinate Lincoln, and that keeping it on one's person would prevent it from doing any more harm. Sophie, to whom Lincoln's death was meaningless compared to the frequent mending she had to do on Paul's trouser pockets, often grumbled that it was a right nasty habit to walk around all day with a pistol in one's pocket. That it was bad luck. It only made us laugh.

*

The next morning we went to Fontenay-le-Fleury for Sacha's wedding. The people of the village had come out en masse to see the procession. The ceremony was very moving, not in and of itself, but because it reminded me of our own wedding. To hear the bride and groom say 'I do' has always had the same effect on me: for a brief moment, love seems so simple – even the least thoughtful, most cynical or disillusioned of the guests believes in it. Only afterwards do people recover their wits, the way Paul did.

'But there's such a big difference in their ages, after all.'

Sacha was fifty-four, Geneviève twenty-five. I didn't say anything, but I did not appreciate his remark at all. It was the second time in less than a week that a difference in age had suddenly loomed up in my life.

The previous Saturday I had seen *Le jour se lève* at the Normandie, and because Carné is far too refined to say it, he had not said it, but the matter is at the very heart of the film. Arletty and Jacqueline Laurent look so much alike that only age sets them apart, and both Gabin and Jules Berry choose the younger woman. Don't say you haven't been warned, Carné must have thought, on hiring the two actresses.

I had pointed this out to the person next to me at the dinner table, who worked in the cinema; this hadn't occurred to him at all upon seeing the film but now that I mentioned it, it stood to reason.

There weren't many of us at the luncheon: one hundred and five, to be exact. Sacha had decided he would invite the same number of people as the number of plays he had written – that was just like him. On the whole I felt at ease. The atmosphere was joyful, the conversation was lively, and this sheltered me from any trivial questions about children. The weather was not good, so we dined inside, except for dessert. In the garden a donkey was pulling a cart in which a cherry tree had been planted, and everyone was to go and help themselves. The women said it was a charming idea, so poetic…The men would have preferred not to have to leave the table, and most of them did indeed skip dessert. The idea of finding myself suddenly surrounded by all those women at the same time frightened me somewhat, and I let them go ahead. It was as I watched them go down the steps of the porch that I suddenly understood they were harmless, my former enemies, and that my adversaries had changed.

Near the donkey pulling its cart was a white doe that Sacha had given Geneviève as a wedding present.

Annie was the beautiful doe and I was the struggling donkey.

The fact of it stunned me. The ten years between us, which I had never really noticed, instantly slapped me in the face.

'Mademoiselle Annie will make a lot of heads turn!'

How many times had Sophie said this to me over these last weeks? I was afraid I was beginning to understand what she had meant by it. You cannot hide a thing from servants, they see what others do not see. We are their centre of interest and even if we are careful, we cannot prevent the incriminating detail from becoming immediately apparent to them. The certain drape of a bedspread, a curtain pulled too tight – only they know how to put things back the way they had left them; a hair that should not be there, behaviour that is overanxious or too distant – they can perceive the slightest changes.

I had got into the car, like every Saturday morning over the last few weeks, but on our way out of the village I acted as if I suddenly remembered the date. They could go on and do the shopping as usual, but I preferred to go home again. Paris on the day after 14 July: the Champs-Elysées would be blocked. So I asked Jacques and Sophie to leave me there at the fork in the road; I would go back on foot.

'Mademoiselle Annie will make a lot of heads turn!'

I clung to those words: I must not change my mind, must not go to back out. Why should I feel embarrassed, after all? I would not be barging in on any sort of intimacy, there wasn't any. I was the one who had laid down the rules for their meetings, so my presence there had nothing indecent about it. I was trying to convince myself of this when I heard the door close behind them. They were going over to the bed. I could not understand what they were saying to each other, their murmuring was muffled by the tapestries. I thought they were lying down. I parted the heavy drapes.

They were not lying down, they were seated. Both of them on the edge of the bed. Paul was running his hand through her hair, revealing her face. Annie had her back to me, I could only see Paul's face, alive, so alive. And then I didn't see him any more, they were kissing. On the lips. Passionately. With her fingers Annie traced the line of Paul's shoulders and neck. He let her; he was looking at her mouth. After their long caresses she went over to the stack of recent canvases on the floor and, after removing the ones on the top, she took one from the middle. A fine hiding place. Before she even had time to put it on the easel I knew what I would see there: Paul's portrait.

She worked for a long spell, with Paul staring straight ahead, unmoving, so peaceful. She put down her brush and came to kneel in front of him. They stayed like that for a long while, speaking quietly. And then he lifted her up and kissed her. They undressed, caressing each other. He took her in his arms, the way one carries a young bride, and set her down on a high stool. He placed his mouth over her sex. She took her pleasure. They returned to the bed, their bodies close together. She sat between his legs, he touched her breasts, her buttocks, kissed her on the forehead, he moaned, she brought him off with her hands, made him come onto the sheets.

So that is what the child I was so hoping for looked like.

They lay down side by side, their hands on each other's sex. Facing each other. Paul helped her to get dressed. He caressed her neck while she tidied her hair. Then they left the room. Hand in hand.

Behind the curtains I vomited, sick with what I had just seen. In my mind their bodies were still entwined, their hands roaming, their mouths biting, giving each other pleasure. But my husband had not penetrated her. They made love in order not to make a child.

But what had I expected? She was so beautiful. And even if she had been less beautiful, her boldness would have made her desirable. She had no modesty, no resistance in her supple body; she was so easy in her manner, so precise in the gestures of her hands; she was erotic, thrilling, even when she lay down, even when she did nothing. I vomited from the knowledge that I would never be able to fight against that, even if I made the same gestures. I vomited with the certainty that my husband was in love with this woman. The body does not err in such cases.

The next morning a strip of white hair ran all along the right side of my head. Paul called out to me just as I discovered this revolting streak. Caught unawares, I quickly covered my head with a scarf. I was afraid he might see it as well and guess, as a result, that I knew everything. He did not even notice the scarf, which was, however, very obvious, being so terribly unfashionable. It was 15 July.

The days went by, stalled in what was only too obvious. Annie's canvases betrayed her betrayal: they were more violent, more tormented. I still remember a field of cornflowers against a black background, filled with a nervous sensuality. As if every flower contained something of Paul's face. It was unbearable. One Saturday followed another and I could say nothing to either of them; I had begged them too often.

And if I had said something to Paul? Would he have chosen me or would he have flung his love for her in my face? I would have liked to say, 'Let's go back to Paris, to our house', but I didn't dare, for fear he might reply, 'Let's take Annie with us.' It would have been unbearable if he had dropped his mask. And if he had not yet confessed to himself that he was in love, there was no need to point it out to him.

I did not try to understand them, but simply to

outfox them, as you always do when you discover a secret that has been deliberately kept from you. I hid more than once behind those heavy drapes. I analysed my husband's gestures, recognising some of the ones he had displayed with me, but above all discovering many others. I needed to see the two of them, to see them loving each other, betraying me, as if I already knew I was about to commit an odious act that required profound hatred. Subsequently, with every moment of weakness or hesitation, those unbearable images took hold and compelled me, inexorably, towards the worst.

We were both in the drawing room. Paul and I. The radio was on, the minister of public health was describing a catastrophic situation: the race to see which country would have the highest birth rate. The German papers were full of examples to follow: 'Schumann was a fifth child, Bach had seven brothers and sisters, Handel nine, Wagner was the youngest of eight children, Mozart of ten...' Here in France the question of the birth rate was of particular concern. The population was declining, you could calculate the figures down to the very moment when France would have lost half its population, then three quarters, and even when it would disappear altogether...

I was not allowed to hear the end. Paul got up nervously and turned the knob on the radio. After a while he said, 'By the way, Annie is still not pregnant.'

I bit my lips to keep from exploding. And yet she takes my husband's member in her mouth.

That year we did not go away on holiday, something which had never happened. We usually spent the summer in our house in Collioure.

*

Paul said the situation in France was too tense, but I knew that was just an excuse. The truth was he did not want to be away from Annie. Not to be outdone, I replied that I too had no plans to leave L'Escalier, given all the riff-raff who were invading our beaches with their paid holidays. And besides, Annie and her parents would surely go away for a few days.

My reaction was such a relief to Paul that he did not even notice my attack on his false pretence, or on Annie, whom I had clearly relegated to her position among the proletarians I so despised. My treachery had no effect: my husband had ceased to view her as a working man's daughter long ago. How could he, playing with her fingers the way he did, kissing her gently in the hollow between her wrist and her hand?

Contrary to all expectation, in mid-August he suggested we go and spend a few days in Deauville; it was not as far away as the south and we could get home more quickly if the situation worsened. What I took to be thoughtfulness on his part turned into a veritable nightmare. You can hide your misfortune in the midst of other unhappy people, but not among happy people. And in contrast to all those individuals who strode along the beach chatting, Paul's misery was striking. He got obsessed by the theft from the Louvre of Watteau's painting, *L'Indifférent*. I recall the title because that was how I felt when the stolen painting was recovered. He read me the articles concerning the theft, Bogousslavsky here, Bogousslavsky there. His monologues terrified me. Not so much because they were virtually the only words my husband addressed to me during our stay, but because they carried the scarcely disguised trace of

*

Annie. It was not to me that he was speaking.

In the toilets of the restaurant where we had lunch I removed my scarf and plucked out my white hairs one by one. By the seventh, I decided that if war was not declared I would murder Annie; by the ninth I was no longer crying, and was plucking them out almost with delight, to the tune of 'Everything is absolutely fine, Madame la Marquise' which I could hear coming from the restaurant.

Separation would be my only salvation. Drowning myself in shameful speculation as to the likelihood of misfortune, I prayed for war with every bone in my body. During the month of August 1939 all the signs were coming together. Civil defence measures were being put in place; sandbags had invaded Paris, covering statues; the Jardin des Plantes had been emptied of its rare animals; and train connections to Germany had been suspended. What others found terrifying was a comfort to me.

War or no war? I clung to the least little hint, even the most specious. Instead of reading the astrologers' predictions, which claimed that, according to the horoscopes of Messrs Hitler and Mussolini, there would be 'no war this summer', I preferred to note that the passage of numerous Bohemian waxwings had been recorded in eastern France and in Germany, as had been the case in 1870 and 1914: these birds, whose feathers are tipped with a sort of splash of blood red wax, are reputed to be the harbingers of great catastrophes. Then there was the rare edition of Nostradamus that had been found and which, similarly, did not predict happy times. 'In 1940 the German armies will invade France from the

*

north and the east. Paris will be reduced to ashes and it is in Poitiers that the definitive battle will be fought. But then a Frenchman will come forward to revive the country's forces and drive the Germans out, and he will be crowned king in Avignon, to universal rejoicing.'

Paul himself had painted an apocalyptic picture of the situation, never realising how happy it made me. Not only would war surely be declared but above all we were bound to lose. There was no point in trying to hide it from me, his newspaper had sent him to investigate the facts regarding military preparedness, and what he had discovered defied commentary. He had managed to intercept some official documents, letters from various members of the military committee, all pointing to defeat: our infantry was inadequate, the cannons were obsolete, the troops were lacking in observational and surveying equipment. There were no tracked munitions supply vehicles, only small lorries that would be incapable of progressing over terrain riddled with shells and mines. Some regiments did not even have any anti-gas materiel, nor any sirens to sound the alarm. And the air force was even worse off. The anti-aircraft artillery could only reach aircraft flying at less than six thousand metres, whereas German planes could reach altitudes of eight to eleven thousand metres. We were desperately short of modern aircraft. The French air force was in danger of being crushed in a matter of days.

Too bad.

I would rather my husband was taken by war than by her.

I would rather my husband was taken by death

*

than by her.

And then there was that ridiculous handshake between Ribbentrop and Molotov. Even Daladier, when they came to wake him in the middle of the night, thought it was a joke on the part of the journalists. But the two schools – war or no war? – continued to face off against each other. There were those who, like Paul, thought that the process had been set in motion and others, like Aragon, who wrote that the war had just receded that bit further, because the pact between the Germans and the Soviets would serve as an instrument of peace against the aggression of the Reich. Errors often arise from certainty.

During the month of August almost all my nights were disturbed by the same dream. I was bombing the Germans and it was thanks to me that war was declared.

On 1 September at four forty-five a.m. the *Schleswig-Holstein*, a German battleship, opened fire on the Polish enclave of Westerplatte. And at eight a.m. Germany proclaimed that Danzig and its territory were henceforth an integral part of the Reich.

At ten thirty Paul woke me up and broke the news to me. He had to go to the recruiting office; a general mobilisation had been ordered. I found no words to reassure him.

We returned to Paris. There were dozens and dozens of children everywhere in the streets, little suitcases or bundles in their hands. Some of them wore large cloth labels with their name across their back. The government had ordered them to be evacuated. I envied all the women who were crying that day: their misery was proof that life had granted them the happiness it so

*

*

obstinately withheld from me.

On 3 September Adolf Hitler got up at seven a.m. and asked for the news from the front. It was excellent: panzers and Stukas were deciding Poland's fate.

At nine fifteen in his study he had the translation of the text of the British ultimatum to Germany read out to him in a loud slow voice.

At twelve thirty the French ambassador in turn delivered the fateful lines: 'The Government of the Republic has the honour of informing the Reich Government that they see themselves in duty bound to fulfil the contractual obligations, as of five p.m. today, 3 September onwards, which they had entered into with Poland and with which the German government is acquainted.'

There was not a single newspaper left in the kiosks. Theatres and cinemas were closed, horse shows were cancelled. Avid crowds hurried to the churches, so numerous that they spilled out onto the church squares. It was raining. Paul and I were at home, in the drawing room, not speaking. Paul was not afraid. He was following events closely. And I was observing him. I would have liked to fix his features in my mind, but those features were dead; another woman had already taken them away.

I went out. It had stopped raining. At the entrances to buildings concierges were painting the word 'shelter' in large white letters. It was nearly five o'clock. All around me men were looking at their watches. Twenty more minutes…Ten more minutes…Five more minutes… The church bell at the Madeleine rang five o'clock. The war had begun.

*

*

One never thinks about those women who were infinitely relieved to see their husbands leaving for war; and yet they did exist, and I was one of them.

The next day, first thing, I asked Jacques to drive me to L'Escalier. I was obliged to go back, otherwise Annie would have realised that I knew something. I owed her at the very least a 'friendly' goodbye. I was sure she would be there, hoping for a miracle, hoping that despite the mobilisation he would be there, too. She was pale. In order to have something to say she told me about her holidays in Dinard, where her father had taken her and her mother.

So that was the real reason why Paul had suddenly wanted to go and 'breathe the sea air'. And to think I had assumed it was for my sake. They certainly did not see one another, otherwise she would not have told me about her trip with such naïveté. It was only the prospect of being a little bit closer to her that had prompted Paul to go to Deauville. That was even worse. How many more lies had he made me swallow?

Above all I would not scream my hatred at her, or tell her that I knew everything; I would not humiliate myself in that way. Just let her be filled with doubt. In the beginning she would not believe me, but the more the days went by, the more the words would gain in strength, and no one would be here to erase them.

I told Annie that the night before he was to leave for the front, Paul broke down. He made me promise to stay in Paris, the mail would get there more quickly; he did not want to abandon me, he loved me with all his soul; he had never been more sure of it than now, in the face of imminent danger; he repeated it to me tirelessly.

*

197

*

He loved me. He loved me. And he made love to me
with all the force of a man in love who is leaving for
war. This had not happened to us for months.

With my words I had just got even with her for all the
hurt she had caused me; I thought I would never see
her again after that.

But at the beginning of October Sophie came into the
library and told me that Annie was asking for me.

'I am pregnant.'

Those words that in the past I had so hoped for now
turned my blood to ice. She was lying. I had seen the
nature of their intercourse; it was not possible.

Annie said nothing else to try and convince me. Her
restraint, her solemn bearing were such that I believed
her.

As if the power of having imagined this moment
so many times were enough to command my body, I
stood up mechanically and went over to embrace her.
I thanked her, told her I was happy. And the most
incredible thing about it was that it was true. I told her
to go home and rest, I would take care of everything. I
had to think of the next step, make a plan.

Obviously I wondered if it was really my husband's
child. What proof did I have that she was only sleeping
with him? But the images I had seen far too often now
came back to me and I was certain she was faithful to
him and that he was the father.

For a moment I was confused. I understood that
they did not want this pregnancy, because it would
inevitably put an end to their trysts. I had no longer
been expecting a child. And then I remembered those
words I had whispered in Annie's ear one day, as if

*

butter wouldn't melt in my mouth. I had insinuated that it might be my husband who was infertile, so perhaps it was useless to persist. My words had wasted no time in finding their way into her womb. That possibility, which I had shared with her without dwelling on it, had sounded threatening. Annie had understood that the arrangement could not continue for ever. So she had managed to find a way to make Paul give her a child after all – the vilest means a woman has at her disposal to keep a man.

I realised soon enough that I had suddenly become mistress of the situation again, and I decided to go back to L'Escalier. I was not sorry to leave Paris. Life during the month of September had been impossible. One could not leave the house without a gas mask, and at the slightest toot of a car horn everyone would feverishly put their gear on, convinced it was an alarm. And then all those sirens in the middle of the night, and going down into the bomb shelters for no good reason, where the worst thing that could happen was getting burgled. Sophie was in a terrible state: her sister had been severely burned during an air-raid drill in the métro; the power had been restored by mistake when there were still passengers on the rails. All the taxis had left Paris to take fleeing families out to the country. I could no longer go out. Everything was closed. Not to mention those who had been mobilised and not yet replaced at their jobs. I was not at all sorry to be going back to L'Escalier.

We would stay in Nuisement so that she would not be far from her parents for too long and, as soon as her pregnancy was about to show, we would go away.

✳

Initially I thought I would take her to Collioure to our holiday home, but as the days went by I became increasingly wary. It would be better, wiser, to go back to Paris.

During the early months of the mobilisation the mail was badly disrupted – it made everyone very angry that letters and packages took weeks to arrive; fortunately for me, otherwise I would have contradicted myself in the course of my letters to Paul. Collioure, Paris, I would have said one thing, then another, and I would have had to justify myself, and thus inevitably arouse his suspicions. But when I received his first letter – on 7 November – I knew exactly what I must do, I had had time to decide my course of action.

It was not enough to hide Annie's pregnancy. I must actually look pregnant myself.

I wrote to Paul:

I was going home, to Paris, and taking Annie with me, I didn't have the heart to leave such a charming person behind. Full stop.

She would keep me company in the course of these very special months. Full stop.

I would never have imagined breaking the news to him like this; we should have been looking into each other's eyes – after all, we were going to have a child. Full stop.

I was pregnant. Full stop.

To vaunt my pregnancy, to make it obvious, was the only way to ensure no one ever came to question my motherhood. I had to protect myself. I did not know what promises they had made to each other during their mad caresses, and I did not want them to be able

*

to claim their word against mine one day.

Fortunately I had not spurned Paul's advances the night before his departure. Even if the declaration of war was an unspeakable relief to me, I was devastated by the thought that I would not see him for months on end, perhaps even long years, or something even worse. So I let him take me in his arms. Perhaps, too, I wanted to be the last one to share his bed, a victory like any other; just because one is scorned does not mean one loses one's pride. What I had told Annie was not a complete lie: Paul did make love to me the night before he left. But not like a man in love who is going to war. Simply like a man who is going to war.

When I suggested to Annie that we go and settle in Paris she immediately agreed. In fact, she agreed to everything over those five months, even to being kept inside the house. Of course I did make it seem as if every one of my decisions had been made with my husband's consent. To win her over to my cause I had no scruples about exploiting the fact she was in love.

As the war was not yet a full-scale one, Paris was now more welcoming once again, and a certain confidence had returned. Mothers who had sent their children to the countryside had them brought back. Only a few people still went down into the shelters; the government itself had reduced the air-raid warnings; and gas masks were added to the pile of things you occasionally tripped over. One fashion designer even decided to use them as a model for a perfume bottle. The trenches in the parks and gardens were used by children playing hide-and-seek. Life had returned to some kind of normality.

*

*

A phoney war for a phoney pregnancy: that is what I said to myself. And what I said to her. I pretended to be as close to her as ever. Dances were allowed again and horse racing, too; nearly all the theatres and cinemas had re-opened. I went out a lot. Because when I was out, I was the pregnant woman, whereas at home I was merely an impostor. But also because it was easier for me to pretend to be expecting a child than to pretend to be fond of Annie.

And yet I did everything in my power to be pleasant and affectionate to her. I told her about the civil code that Daladier had just created, and the allowance of three thousand francs granted to each firstborn child. I was very careful with what I told her, I knew very well that she had not agreed to bring this child into the world for money, but the sum in question was hers by rights. And I enticed her with the thought of all the canvases and brushes and charcoals she'd be able to afford with that money. All of which was meant to forestall any inclination she might have to go back on her word or run away.

I kept a close watch on her. Although it may have seemed that our trust was well-established, and that she did not mind being locked up, I had asked Sophie to keep her well within sight, to be always aware of Annie's whereabouts.

I even gave her a kitten, imagining that in her solitude she would pour her unhappy heart out to the little creature, and that her passionate and soppy words might help me to learn more about her and my husband. But she spoke only to her belly, and even then so quietly that Sophie could not detect the slightest word.

*

*

And if by chance Annie tried to leave the house, the front door, which was always locked, would have prevented her. But deep down I always knew she would stay; my best ally in preventing her from leaving was Paul. She was waiting for him.

Whenever I received a letter from him, I took malicious delight in informing Annie of the fact and giving her a brief summary of his news. How her eyes shone when I talked to her about Paul; she no longer breathed the same way, she was physically hanging on my every word. It hurt to see the way she looked at me. Sometimes, sadistically, I purposely did not tell her what she was hoping to hear. But then I would change my mind a few hours later when I saw how her face had clouded over, how sad and distant she had become. I did not want to inflict such a mood upon the baby she was carrying, my baby, so I would say to her, 'Oh by the way, Annie, I forgot to tell you, my husband sends you his regards.'

At the end of each of his letters, Paul added a post scriptum: 'Say hello to Annie for me.' This short sentence, always the same, tarnished every message I received from him. Distance had made him gentler with me, as had the prospect of the baby; he asked me a lot of questions which I was always careful to answer – once I had asked Annie. His letters were long, because even at the front where nothing was happening, my husband was still a journalist. But in spite of our renewed complicity, that unchanging post scriptum, a razor sharp sword of Damocles, proved to me with every letter that that girl had not left his thoughts. And I imagined him composing the final sentence with so much more care

*

than all the others. 'Say hello to Annie for me.'

For my part, in my letters, I always gave him some brief news about Annie.

I often wondered if they would have written to each other if she had not been at the house with me. I was, alas, all too certain of the truth.

And then one day a telegram came unexpectedly, without a post scriptum.

```
at last stop will be there twenty-
second march stop six days leave at
last stop
```

Six days' leave, the end of everything.

Under normal circumstances Paul would have said 'a week', but in these troubled times, a day was a day and approximation was no longer part of our way of thinking. Danger makes one precise. I was in a complete panic. 'Will be there twenty-second.' In these troubled times, in particular, nothing was less reliable than a date, time had lost its meaning; the war, however phoney, was imposing its own rhythm. That of fickleness. Of unpredictable variability. It was 18 March. Things could have changed a thousand times since he wrote that telegram. His leave might have been brought forward, to suit some mission or one of his company comrades. He could easily arrive today, from one minute to the next. Or he might even have invented that date in order to surprise me and show up unexpectedly from one minute to the next.

I imagined him disembarking from the train. Paying for the taxi. I imagined him standing before me with a

*

smile that meant, 'Here I am!' The slightest little sound terrified me, here he was! I ordered Sophie to pack our cases for a few days and to prepare some supplies. She asked me where we were going. I myself did not know, and replied curtly that she did not need to know in order to pack, it ought to be enough that I had ordered her to! Poor Sophie. As far as I was concerned, danger had made me more aggressive than precise.

I had never wanted to entertain the possibility that Paul could be granted leave. Every day already brought with it its share of 'real' events which I had to deal with, so that I refused to envisage those which might 'possibly' occur. Everything was already so complicated that I wanted to believe he would never be granted leave.

We went away that very night. To the mill. Even if my husband visited all our properties, never for a moment would he imagine we could be there; the place was too uncomfortable, too Spartan. Annie did not mind. I had presented this sudden escapade as an idea of my husband's, to 'give the baby some fresh air'. How lucky we were! We would be able to celebrate springtime in the heart of the countryside. Annie continued to go along with everything as if it were all completely normal.

'And Alto?'

'What about Alto?'

We had been driving for a long time already when we turned back to fetch the cat. Its fate had not crossed my mind for an instant.

Paul would never come and look for us here; it was the sort of destination one ran away to, and he would

∗

never suspect I was running away from him. I spent two weeks cloistered in the smell of wheat, trying to convince myself of that. I was terrified at the thought that Paul might suddenly show up and confront me. Finland had surrendered to the Russians a few days before our departure. I had no way of knowing what was going on at the front. What if events suddenly took a turn for the worse and we were trapped here unawares?

In all those months, the days at the mill were without a doubt the most gruelling. My fears were so violent that I talked in my sleep. I slept with Annie and I was afraid I might give myself away. Eventually I moved into the kitchen and onto Sophie's mattress.

I had never been so unsure of my plans. Was it the solitude? Or the silence and idleness? I had almost forgotten how much the two of them had hurt me. I tried to revive my grievances against them, but they almost left me indifferent. The only feelings that lingered were guilt and remorse. And I even wondered, would I be a good mother? Would I be loved in return? My husband must be looking for me at that very moment, but not for my sake. Perhaps this child would not love me, either. Perhaps I was simply not a lovable person.

I think I could have given it all up but they had aroused my dormant anger once again.

I was afraid to go back to Paris and find Paul still there; the date of his departure could also have been delayed. I had no choice, I had to go and see for myself. I could not send Jacques to check whether Monsieur had gone to join his regiment; I did not want him to find out about Annie's pregnancy. I feared nothing on the part of Sophie, but from Jacques, yes. He always said, 'Oui, Madame', 'Oui, Monsieur', before we had even finished our sentences. It wasn't overzealousness, but an imperious need to be part of the action. He was far too impulsive to keep a secret. He had other qualities, but with him anything was possible. Nowadays, if I am to believe what people have told me, he's an elderly gentleman and he is doing well. Fortunately I left him out of this whole business; everyone else who was involved has died in far too tragic a way.

That was the only day I regretted not confiding in him, because it left me no choice, I had to go and see for myself whether Paul had left.

I waited for a few days beyond the scheduled date for the end of his leave and, without even telling Sophie, I set off on the road for Paris. I arrived at the house at around midnight. There were no lights on anywhere. This was a good sign: as a rule, my husband was never asleep at this hour. He might have gone out, but in all likelihood he was in his blockhouse with the other soldiers. I tried to reassure myself, but my heart was in my boots when I opened the door.

I immediately saw his letter. It was there on the credenza in the entrance, visible in the moonlight.

Where was I? Hadn't I received his telegram? He hoped I was doing well. He was so sorry we had not seen each other. How unlucky could one be? And the baby, he would have so loved to feel it beneath his fingers, to see my belly moving. He was so worried about the future. One mustn't have illusions, the present lack of military engagement could not last. There would be real fighting soon and, given the motorised nature of

✲

warfare, it would be far more ghastly than the Great War. We must prepare for the worst. He could not understand why the government left so many soldiers at the front where nothing was happening when there was such a shortage of workers in the factories. You just have to see that the carrot peeler in their regiment was a 'mechanical fitter' of aeroplane engines. It was a mixed-up world. He apologised for talking to me about all that, he would so much have preferred me to experience my pregnancy under better circumstances. He begged us to take care of ourselves, and of the baby; he was so sorry not to have seen us, he had looked for us everywhere. He kissed me and held me close, in his arms – were they not already too short to circle my round belly?

I might have found his long message touching had he not written 'yourselves'. And above all, had I not read yet another message.

During the days at the mill I no longer had the strength to bluff. In order not to give anything away to Annie, or allow her to be vexed by my mood, I found a solution: crossword puzzles. They allowed me to think out loud without having to pretend I had no worries. So while Annie thought I was busy figuring out my 'Across' and 'Down' clues, I was constantly thinking about the situation, turning the future this way and that, working through every possibility. I had envisaged this very moment, I had imagined myself folding Paul's letter as I headed up to the next floor, not even bothering to take off my coat. I had known he would leave me a letter in plain sight somewhere. What I hadn't known was whether he would mention Annie or not.

∗

*

He had not mentioned her. Not a word. No post scriptum.

Had his despair at not seeing me made him forget Annie? Had he realised the extent of the wrong he had done? Had he come back to me? Or, on the contrary, had he managed to get word to her without going through me? Had he written a letter just for her?

If so, he would have given a lot of thought as to where to hide it. He might have slipped it beneath one of the parquet boards initially. But no sooner would he have put the board back in place than he would worry. What if Annie did not look that carefully? Even if he left the floorboard somewhat loose, it would not suffice as a clue. No, it was too risky. It would be better to leave the letter in a place where Annie would be sure to find it as she went about her daily business. So, he would stick it beneath her palette. And then, once again, he would be anxious. What if she was no longer painting? Or not every day – after all, he knew nothing about her new habits. No, that was too risky. What intimate gesture could he be really sure of?

I pulled back the sheets and the letter was there, exactly where I knew it would be. Paul was so eager to have her read it that he had become foolhardy, careless.

Anyone could find it there, without even looking. Paul had taken an incredible risk. Because the risk, for him, was not that someone else might find that letter, but that Annie might fail to find it.

He thought of her day and night, he wrote. It was a veritable torture not to be able to see her or speak to her or write to her. He had waited so long to obtain his leave all for nothing. But at least he could leave these words

*

for her. He hoped we were reading his letters together, because they were also addressed to her, he hoped she had realised that. It was also for her sake that he described his days. So that she could imagine him there if she wanted to. So that she would have the impression she was with him, in a way, if she wanted to. He worried about her. Was she happy? He was so sorry to hear about her father. He had heard the news when he went to look for us in the village. But everything would work out, it was only a matter of weeks. They couldn't hold him prisoner for ever, not for such a minor thing. Was she still painting? Was she painting things she liked? He had spent a lot of time in her bedroom over the last six days, looking at her canvases. Her colours had become more beautiful, more exact or intense, he couldn't find the word. He had touched every object; he had sat on the chair, lain on the bed, to feel closer to her. Looking for us, he had gone round all the shops in the neighbourhood in case one of them knew where we were; and the idea that they knew her was a comfort to him, he even felt himself grow hard with pride at the thought that they must have found her beautiful. He lived to desire her; he often did what they had murmured to each other before his departure. And what about her? Did she do it? Did she dare? He loved her. He loved her. He had just heard Reynaud's inauguration speech on the radio: 'Win and you save everything, succumb and you lose everything.' Not when you succumbed to her. He embraced her with his whole body.

I held two envelopes in my hands. On one, Paul had written, 'Elisabeth'. On the other, 'My love'. Things could scarcely be any clearer.

✳

I might have chosen to overlook a child, but not an adulterous love affair. I had almost abandoned everything; now it was out of the question. I had finally understood what I had to give up, and what I could still fight. They could go to the devil. The child would be mine. That was all I had left. A betrayed woman is a mother in the making.

On 9 April 1940 when I told her that Hitler was invading Denmark and Norway, Annie felt unwell. 'Just contractions,' she said, to reassure me, 'all of a sudden, my belly moves upwards and turns as hard as a stone', but it wasn't serious, she said.

Perhaps. But when I saw Annie collapse suddenly on the ground, her hands on her belly, her breathing erratic, I thought she was having a miscarriage, and I was so afraid that I decided then and there not to tell her anything more that might upset her or even worry her. I knew she was afraid that the war was gearing up into serious fighting, and that Paul's life would now be in real danger. If he were to disappear, not only would she be full of sorrow for her lost love – which was of little import to me – but Annie would have no one to stop me from taking her baby, and she knew it. Even if she acted as if this were not the case, the prospect was unbearable.

To give up her child after having carried it was already wrenching enough, and now that it was her love child…that nuance changed everything, and I had understood this long ago. I may have lacked certain physical qualities for procreation, but my maternal instinct was intact all the same. Women should always be deprived of both at once; that would prevent untold episodes of sorrow and tragedy.

✱

I became the censor of all censors and only told her about the musical instruments sent to the soldiers, the cards, books, the hundred thousand footballs they had received, or the credit of three million francs that had been released for the purchase of jerseys, because there were so many football enthusiasts at the front…If Annie were to believe me alone, the war was one huge charity ball and nothing else.

I dreamed of hurting her, but I wanted her to remain a happy womb for my child. I had always heard that the happier the pregnancy was, the happier the child would be, so I tried to keep her calm. I made numerous promises that I did not believe in: nothing would change after the birth, she would stay with us, she would always be able to see her baby and look after it and later, when it was old enough to understand, then we would see; we might try and explain things.

That is what I told her, very calmly, on 10 May when the Germans invaded. A lie equal to the drama that was unfolding. A poultice equal to the wound that was being inflicted upon us. On the pretext of bringing a bouquet of flowers to her room, I clumsily spilled the water from the vase all over the wireless. She must not be exposed to the turmoil of these past weeks; censorship continued to keep a great deal from us but what it did reveal was more than enough to overwhelm her. I wanted the baby to be born, that was all I could think of.

I saw so many refugees heading off. Magnificent American cars speeding by, liveried chauffeurs bent over their road maps. And older, less stylish cars, filled with families. Then came the bicycles and people

∗

on foot, women wearing hats and their Sunday best, sweating under the multiple layers of clothing they had piled on to be able to take as much as possible with them.

In spite of the panic, I had never once thought of leaving: Annie might give birth at any moment.

On the night of 15th her first contractions began. After a few hours had gone by the situation degenerated and Sophie asked me to go and fetch a doctor. Annie was screaming, writhing in pain. She was gasping and wheezing, hoarse. She could not bear to be on her back and was on the floor on all fours, like an animal. But I couldn't do it. At the wheel of my car, I kept thinking, I cannot go for a doctor, no one must know it is her baby. The moon was full and bathed the streets in a white light. I drove with all my lights off, no dipped or side lights. But I had been right to go out. The hope that I was going to come back with a doctor would help her more than if I had stayed there, useless and vicious, hypnotised by her pain. She would have seen that my feelings were not equal to the situation. I felt neither fear nor distress at the sight of her suffering, that's just how it was, empathy stops where rivalry begins.

I don't know how many times I went over that same route, perhaps a hundred times. A madwoman's circus. From home to home again, by way of Pasquin's house. When I came alongside his building I slowed down, swearing upon the memory of my parents that if I saw that dear doctor entering or leaving his house I would call out to him, but no one appeared. So back I went to the house where, once again, I did not stop, for fear of what Sophie would have to tell me – deliverance? Or tragedy? So I set off for Pasquin's yet again, certain this time that I would find him outside his house. There was no reason why I should, but as I no longer possessed my powers of reason, anyway...Sophie would hand the child to me, Annie had died in childbirth. I let the words echo through my mind over and over, like a waltz, 'died in childbirth', 'died in childbirth', it would have made everything so much easier. I was laughing and crying at the same time, because I knew that her death could also take my baby with her. Does Death always use the same scythe to kill, or is there one scythe per person? And Pasquin was still not outside his house...

And all these cars being loaded in haste, lorries cascading with archives and boxes and papers of all sorts that must not fall into the hands of the enemy. Civil servants fleeing, a silent, nocturnal disintegration. The moon terrified me, it was in a phase where you could easily see a face there, and I had the impression it was following my every movement. I explained to the moon that it could not understand me, that it could not possibly know what it is to want a child so badly. And then I thought of how the moon is often viewed as female: perhaps because its body also changes shape depending on the time of the month. Did each full moon give birth to a star? And what if the moon were the mother of all the stars? I kept on driving, long after it had disappeared. And Pasquin was still not outside his house...

Then I saw huge flames rising from the gardens at the Quài d'Orsay. It was this raging fire that finally shocked me out of my torpor. Had I, by dint of going back and forth past the same place, been the match that had finally lit the blaze? There were not enough lorries;

✳

all the compromising documents had to be burned on the spot. Black smoke and paper ash rose into the sky. I remember thinking that I did not like dead matches. It was time to go home.

Sophie handed me the baby. Annie had fallen asleep. To appropriate the words of all the new mothers on earth: 'I will remember this instant all my life.' I melted into Camille's eyes; they were open, glassy. It was not really what you would call a gaze, but it would be my life from then on. I stayed like that for a long time, sitting there, Camille against my breast. And my greatest fear had not been realised, she did not look like Annie. Dear God, thank you.

The days went by, numb, sweet. Naturally the surrender of Holland and Belgium upset me, naturally I was shaken by the German advance, but I withdrew into the scent of my little girl. I could not help it, everything that was happening around me washed over me. The miracle of her birth coloured everything and convinced me that even this war would be resolved by a miracle. And wasn't the Maréchal's return already a miracle of a kind?

The other miracle was that I no longer saw Annie with the same eyes. The German attack had rearranged my circle of adversaries – Annie still belonged there, but not as much as she previously had. The Germans had taken some of my hatred from her. It was mathematical: the more enemies you have – or at least, the more you think you have – the less virulent the hatred you bear them. Whatever people may say, hatred, like love, is not inextinguishable.

And I saw Annie looking at Camille, I saw the mother

taking possession of her child. How could I possibly have thought of taking the child away from her? How could she have thought of giving her up to me? Our moods when we were alone or in each other's presence were now a thing of the past. Her ambition as a painter and my despair as an infertile woman had faded in the light of Camille's brand new life. Our lives had stopped to make room for Camille's life; this period immediately after the birth precluded any need to make decisions other than to feed and change the newborn child and lull her to sleep. It was a remarkable time. Annie was nursing Camille, I could not. I changed her, rocked her, Annie could not. And everything seemed to be just the way it should be.

If Annie had confessed everything to me in the course of those few days, if she had asked for my forgiveness, had asked me for her daughter, I would have let the two of them go away together, however much it might have cost me. It is easy for me to say that now, but I swear that, with the benefit of hindsight, I still believe it. In every conflict there is always a moment when two rivals see eye to eye, and if at that opportune moment they could just be open to each other, instead of continuing to sniff around each other warily, an undreamed-of agreement might ensue.

Instead, Annie asked me if I had sent the little booties to Paul.

I had knitted two pairs, one blue and one pink, and we had agreed that I would 'send Paul the colour that was born'. Annie liked to use that expression, probably because a colour seemed to belong more to her than to her child.

*

I had consented, without daring to tell her that they had just announced that the soldiers at the front could no longer receive packages. The situation was getting worse by the day, but I continued to surround Annie with an aura of well-being. It had become a habit and, above all, I did not want her milk to dry up; she had had a difficult birth and now Camille had to thrive.

But Paul would have been happy to see the colour, he so wanted to have a little girl, 'so that she will never have to go to war', as he often said in his letters. I had been dreaming of a boy, because I thought there was less likelihood he would look like Annie…And above all because a boy never has to acknowledge, one fine day, that he cannot have a child. One always wants to avoid the worst for one's child.

But on 3 June, when the Germans dropped their bombs a few streets from ours, I had to tell Annie that the war had broken out in earnest.

'It was a suicide attack' which 'attested to the Germans' despair,' and 'to show how inane their offensive was, the government was still in Paris and had no intentions of leaving.'

The stoic tone of the opinion columns in the newspapers had been more efficient than the best lies I could have invented. I gave no further details to Annie, and she did not ask for any; she too was completely absorbed by Camille.

I decided I would not leave Paris, no matter what, and I never strayed from that decision. Even when Reynaud, the government, and all the ministers

*

eventually fled like cowards and left a seething capital city in their wake, and hundreds of thousands of panicked Parisians rushed onto the streets.

It was 10 June. We heard that the Germans were less than fifteen kilometres away, and that the Italians had just come into the war on their side. Almost all my friends and acquaintances had fled, and some of them had suggested I go with them, begging me not to stay on my own with my baby. But it was the opposite that frightened me: I thought it would be lethal to take a newborn child into that stampede.

The only outings I enforced were our daily walks. I liked nothing better than those moments when, as a couple, we walked the streets and parks, amongst the trees and the pecking of the pigeons. The shopkeepers – those who hadn't fled – would lean over the pram to inhale a little bit of optimism: we would not be able to lose the war if babies kept being born. Depending on the day, they might inform me that the United States had declared war on Germany, or that a major French counter-offensive was being mounted with an exceptional reserve army, or that Hitler was very ill and might be abdicating in favour of Goering, then they would look up from the pram and say kindly, 'It is extraordinary how much your baby looks like you.' One absurd statement after another, to reassure themselves and me. And how we all wanted to believe in them.

There were people everywhere in the streets. They made me think of animals in flight, determined yet lost. I could not help but despise them; they seemed cowardly.

And then one day I saw him, too.

*

*

I immediately recognised him, despite his beard and his dishevelled hair; I recognised that arrogant air of his. His face was as inscrutable as on the day I had met him, his attitude still that of a braggart. At first it was the bystanders' cries that had drawn my attention; they were screaming their heads off, insulting a group of prisoners who were clustered on the other side of the street opposite the Café Piémont. 'Bastards!' 'Hooligans!' 'Layabouts!' Three of their guards, who had obviously had more than a drink or two, were harassing the detainees who were asking for a glass of water.

'If you're thirsty, take a piss and drink that!'

'Go on, move along, stinking scum!'

They too were part of the exodus: they had to be transferred to another prison. I waited for the group to draw level with me and then I called to the guard who was bringing up the rear. I asked him if he would like some money. His eyes lit up, but he looked at me in silence, waiting to find out what the matter was. I had two hundred francs on me, they would be his if he let him go. He grabbed the notes out of my hand and murmured that, besides, given the way things were going, if he didn't let him go then the Boches would, so he might as well...He cleared his throat noisily before spitting on the ground.

'Why that one?'

'Because he's an old man.'

'There's plenty of old men.'

'Because he looks like my daughter's grandfather.'

I pointed to the pram which I was still rocking with one hand, a rhythm that nothing could interrupt. 'I

*

get it,' he said, then shrugged his shoulders and went away, stuffing the money into his pocket. I didn't wait to see if he released him, I'd done what seemed to be the right thing, the rest had nothing to do with me. I felt as if I had redeemed myself.

I wanted to tell Annie that her father was free, but I had never been able to bring myself to tell her that he had been arrested. She would have wanted to leave, to go and be with her mother, I could not have held her back and I would have had to say farewell to my baby. Nevertheless, I had asked Jacques to make sure that the old woman had everything she needed. He told me that there was a young lad who stopped by to see her nearly every day. This made me feel less guilty; she was not completely alone.

I acted badly, I concede. But she in turn must not have loved her daughter very much, for she did not write her a single letter during that entire period. At the same time I was not really surprised, nothing in the world would have made her jeopardise her daughter's relation with a 'rich woman', and she surely hoped to gain from it in one way or another. There is no one more abject than a poor relation when money is at stake.

Sophie was the one who came to warn me that Paris was an 'open city', that there were posters everywhere; no one knew exactly what that meant but everyone knew it was a bad sign. We felt that something terrible was about to happen. It was 12 June 1940. The rumour had spread that the Germans were coming.

The next evening, while I was in my bath, the power was cut, and I was plunged into complete darkness. I groped my way to Annie's room to make sure everything was all right. She had fallen asleep and Camille was babbling in her cradle. I searched the chest of drawers, one drawer after another, looking for candles; it was nearly time for the baby's next feed, and Annie would need some light. I rummaged through her things as best I could and thought I had found what I needed beneath her handkerchiefs. But it was colder than a candle, and made of metal. No bigger than a child's toy. I remember giving a weary, almost incredulous cry as I took it out from under the pile of cloth.

Proof that their love affair was going stronger than ever. Would it never end?

'Leaving you this pistol is my promise that I shall come back to you...'

'To the most precious woman in my life, I bequeath the most precious object in my life...'

I spent the night imagining all the vows Paul must have made on leaving 'the little Derringer' to Annie before he went away to war. Perhaps he handed it to her in silence before they made passionate love. No doubt.

I awoke with a start to find the gun on my pillow, the barrel pointed towards me. I felt weak, more tired than before going to sleep. I was doing my hair when Sophie burst into the bathroom. 'They're here!' People had seen them. I sent her to the cellar at once, to put together some reserves and set up the bedding we had already taken down as a precaution, including Camille's cradle – in case they began to pillage, in case we had to hide. And I went back to brushing my hair mindlessly. I felt oppressed. The Germans were here. People had seen them. I felt the Derringer in the pocket of my bathrobe,

*

banging against my hip with every stroke of my brush. I heard a sudden noise and swivelled around, panic-stricken. Alto had just come in and jumped on the edge of the bathtub, strolling along with his feline gait. I don't know what came over me, I can't explain it, I could not take my eyes off him. I put my brush down carefully, felt for the gun in my pocket, took aim, and pressed the trigger.

'Fuck off and leave me alone, all of you!'

When the gun went off I thought my arm was being wrenched out of its socket. I don't know if I cried out. Alto's body flipped into the bath and the water was saturated with blood in a matter of seconds. A sour taste came to my mouth. I did nothing. I watched him struggle without reacting. I saw myself in the bath again, the day I told Annie everything. Alto drowned the way a human being does, without making a sound. If I had not told her anything, none of this would have happened. When Alto stopped moving I no longer recognised his body covered with wet fur.

I could still hear the gunshot echoing in my brain. Alto's body, floating. I could not understand how it could have happened. Paul had never left any of his collection pieces loaded, including the Derringer. The ammunition had always lain dormant in a drawer in his desk, all mixed up together. Sophie used to say, 'A mother cat couldn't even find her kittens in there...'

Nor would Paul have loaded the pistol before giving it to her, it wasn't his way; for him these weapons were mere mementos. He cherished them because they had belonged to his father, but he no longer viewed them as weapons.

*

222

*

But who else might have loaded that gun if he hadn't?

The answer came to me like a bolt of lightning. Annie, trying all the bullets, one after the other, with patience and determination, until she found the one that fitted perfectly in the barrel. And then she added the powder. Everything was ready.

Because my desire for revenge obsessed me, I had never considered her own hatred towards me. Yet she had been thinking of killing me: you don't load a gun just because you're bored. What had held her back? Had I escaped the worst, or had she, like me, lacked the courage to kill?

I felt a sort of rush. Everything had to stop. Now. Our strange companionship could not last much longer. Camille was a month old. She still went from one pair of arms to another without minding, but soon she would begin to smile for one of us in particular and call her 'Maman', and I wanted that person to be me.

Giving birth is a mysterious thing, it removes a woman from society for a while and then suddenly returns her to it, just like that, abruptly. After weeks of stupor and bliss one becomes active again, one becomes the person one was before, in a denser, more concentrated fashion, not necessarily for the better, because now one is fighting not just for oneself but also for one's child. With that single gunshot, life had just reasserted its rights over the privileged era of new motherhood.

I went into Annie's bedroom, took Camille from her arms and locked myself away with her in my room. Camille was crying, but it hardly mattered, I was not upset, even for her; I felt nothing but a heavy mass in my chest. The shock had been so violent that

*

223

I was breathing hard through my nose. I could not understand what had happened. I never suspected the Derringer was loaded.

It was Camille's first bottle. To begin with she did not want it but eventually she came round. I could hear Annie knocking on the door, running everywhere, calling for help. I put Camille on the rug on the floor, left the room, locking it behind me, and went downstairs. Annie asked me what I had done with her baby. My manner was as cold as hers was agitated. I replied that I did not know what she was talking about, insofar as she had no baby, and then I said, viciously:

'Paul has confessed to everything, I know all about the two of you, how you used to meet.'

I described their lovemaking to her, using the most intimate words, the most explicit, too, unbearable even for someone who lacked modesty. She listened, shaking her head from left to right as if she were saying, no, no, in her head. Then she blocked her ears with shame and humiliation. I had imagined her collapsing in sobs but her eyes stayed dry. Tears make one lose one's concentration, and she had to be on her guard and listen. Attentiveness prevailed over despair.

'And that afternoon when he showed you what you had to do while you waited for him, when he told you to lie on the bed and pull up your skirt, and took the fingers of your left hand, and, after kissing them, placed them in that precise spot at the top of your sex between the two lips, while his other hand was on your breasts. He sat naked next to you. His sex was hard and he asked you to look at it. He did not touch you. He merely murmured to you what you had to do. You

*

complied; you were filthy and obedient. You rubbed the spot where your fingers lay, gently at first and then faster and faster, harder and harder, your eyes glued to his sex. And then you gave a moan and arched your back before your body finally yielded, trembling, and Paul took you in his arms and rocked you like a little girl. "Will you dare to do it when I'm not here?"'

I gave her the details in such a way that she could not fail to believe they came from my husband. She could not suspect the truth, that I lay in ambush only a few metres from them, stiff and hateful, in the folds of the heavy drapes. I wanted to defile their intimacy for ever, deprive her of the pleasure she had taken with my husband, even in her memories. Never again would she be able to think of their embraces without imagining Paul confessing to me, telling me that those embraces meant nothing to him, that for those few months he had gone astray, but now he begged me to forgive him.

I had envisaged that confrontation for so long. I had thought it through, preparing every little word, always choosing the most perfidious. To make Annie flee, to fill her with despair. To prevent her from pouring out her misfortunes to anyone who was prepared to listen, showing her body, still swollen from the birth, as proof. A doctor would not hesitate for one second to declare which of our two bodies had just given birth and which had never been anything but an empty shell. I had to humiliate her so thoroughly that I would drain her of the energy it would take to seek a doctor's testimony; I had to render that testimony null and void, utterly inadmissible.

I had lied to her. As I said this Annie sat up, questioning, hoping I would suddenly refute everything I had just said and give her a new, less horrendous version.

'Yes, I lied to you. Paul never sent his regards, in any of his letters. I told you what you wanted to hear, for my child's welfare. Oh, yes! Because I forgot to tell you, Paul was so happy to learn that I was pregnant. He could not stop saying how happy he was that we would be a family at last. We deserved it so much, after all we had been through…Mark my words, when a man loses his family in one of life's tragedies – as Paul has done – all he thinks of is starting a new one. Even the least gregarious individual needs the support of a family. Mistresses – and mark this, too, for your next bout of whoring – are good for men who see a member of their family wherever they look; others need to build a family, that's the way it goes…Sex is stronger than men, to be sure, but family is stronger than anything.'

The door slammed behind her. At last. It was over.

Murder is an alliance of circumstances and temperament, and while we both had the circumstances, neither of us had the temperament. I had thought of killing her, too, a thousand times, but in the end I resorted to nothing more than throwing her out. The most refined hatred, if it is not armed with a murderous temperament, will never kill a soul.

No sooner had the door slammed behind her than I already regretted that my desire to have her out of my sight had been stronger than caution, which would have required keeping her at hand.

In the weeks that followed, a paranoid fear took hold of me. Her absence turned out to be far more menacing

*

than her presence. What was she going to do now? Had she believed my lies? Would she go on waiting for Paul? And Camille? Would she give her up all the same? There was nothing I could be sure of.

I had asked Jacques to stay at L'Escalier, officially as a caretaker, but in reality to keep an eye on Annie, who, Jacques confirmed, had gone back to Nuisement. But knowing where she was did not reassure me altogether. When Jacques informed me that her mother had died, I was indecently pleased. From now on, I thought, Annie would stay put, to look after her father.

Sophie lectured me: there were things one could do legitimately in life, and other things that were just not done – what would I say if one day someone behaved like that towards my daughter? Annie's charm did not act exclusively upon men; I was in a good position to know, I too had succumbed to it at one time and I think that Sophie was very fond of her. But she was entirely devoted to me. I never understood how she could support me in this undertaking, it was everything she despised: lies, betrayal, theft.

I had advised her to leave, it was getting too risky for her. I told her that there were many Jews also swelling the numbers of those who were fleeing. I was not one of those who despised them, but I had read the articles in the newspapers which seemed to promise the worst where they were concerned. Those who say that in those days we knew nothing about the camps are liars. But Sophie simply did not want to know. She would not leave me until Monsieur came home, she had promised him she would look after me, her word was her bond.

*

And she was French above all else, and if the French needed her to make life difficult for the Germans, she would be there. I should just call her Marie, like all the other maids in Paris; and if you looked closely, didn't her nose look like a pretty little Breton nose? The Germans would be none the wiser.

I should never have let her make me laugh and win me over, I should have ordered her to leave right away. In the end she was the one who was none the wiser.

They showed up one morning, very early, two plain-clothes German policemen. And their usual despicable scenario played out before my eyes. It wasn't an arrest; they just wanted to 'take a statement' at the police station, and after that in all likelihood she would be able to come home, but they suggested she take a bag with some belongings anyway. They watched her as she got ready, and when she went to the toilet, one of the policemen wedged his foot in the door so she could not close it. I never understood how they had managed to find her. In spite of her pretty little Breton nose I had not been allowing her out of the house for several months; I did the shopping myself and she stayed at home to look after Camille and the housework. She hadn't even been opening the door any more if the bell rang. Someone, an acquaintance, perhaps, must have denounced her as a Jew.

Oh, how she kissed Camille before she left. She whispered a few sweet words in her ear, and her eyes were shining with tears and rage, but she controlled her emotions. She held the child so tight against her breast that one of the policemen abruptly took me to one side:

'This is your child, isn't it, Madame?'

*

Those words I had so feared, now asked at such an inappropriate and painful moment, made me laugh nervously. Sophie turned to me, not understanding.

'I'm laughing, Marie, because Monsieur is asking me to assure him that Camille is not your daughter.'

A kindly smile lit up Sophie's face, and that is the last image I have of her.

The months went by, somewhat more calmly, until that day in December when someone rang at the door. From Jacques' description, I immediately recognised the young boy who had been visiting Annie's mother every day during our absence. He looked exactly how I had imagined him. Annie had left Nuisement the day before and he thought she must be here. At first I thought it was a ruse to try and take Camille back by force. The dismay I saw in his eyes when I told him Annie was not here reassured me. It was not a trap; he really was looking for her. I hadn't ever thought to invent an explanation for Annie's absence, but it was his manner, that lovesick air of his that inspired the unbearable story I told him: that Annie had fallen in love with a soldier. I even went so far as to say they were married. May he forgive me.

He left, devastated. And I was relieved. Annie had not told him anything about her relationship with my husband. I thought the danger had passed until he adopted that voice people use to speak to babies.

'Goodbye, Louise.'

Annie was the only one who knew that name: he had just given himself away. He knew the truth, at least as far as Camille was concerned.

*

*

When Annie had suggested we call the baby Louise, I had pretended to go along with it: at the time, I pretended to go along with everything. But deep down I always wanted the child to have my mother's name, Camille. She had to have something of me, after all. I did not hesitate for one second when I went to see the registrar.

'Camille Marguerite Werner.'

Nor in response to the following question.

'Date of birth?'

'Five days ago: the twenty-eighth of June.'

Camille was a little older than one month, but I said she was born 'five days ago', like almost all the other new mothers ahead of me in the queue. As a rule when they got to the window, the fathers would say, 'yesterday', but now with the war it was the women who said 'five days ago', or 'a week ago', depending on how long it had taken them to recover from the birth.

I wasn't risking anything; soon enough, over time, no one would notice a month. Annie must have no official truth about Camille in her possession. So that my child would be a stranger to her, and remain so for ever. Paul, too, always believed his daughter was a month younger than she actually was. I was alone, in my heart, wishing Camille happy birthday on the real day of celebration, just as, over the years, as aging went hand in hand with guilt, I had the misery of my past lies to celebrate alone.

'Goodbye, Louise.'

I watched as the young man left, feeling a strange compassion for him. He and I shared something in this story; we had both been betrayed, scorned, rejected.

*

*

But he knew that Camille was Annie's child, and in that respect he was a threat. I had to keep an eye on him, I had to be able to circumvent the danger. He also seemed like the best way of finding Annie. If she showed up again somewhere, it would be for his sake, of that I was sure. They shared something special. The kind of love that inspires a woman to choose that man's name for her child, when he cannot be the father. To be sure of him, I kept a constant watch on his whereabouts.

So Annie had left Nuisement, and could reappear at any moment. And what if she and Paul came hand in hand to take Camille from me? Did they really exist, those women who were so in love that they went to Germany to look for their imprisoned lovers?

We were late for the puppet show. Camille had just turned one. I sat her down on the bench in front and left her there while I went to buy a ticket. The kiosk was just nearby. It was as I was returning to my seat that I saw Annie silhouetted against a tree. Her face lit up at Camille's every move and she laughed along with her. Children laugh from their chest, like a cry, and adults from their throat, like a sigh; and when they happen to laugh the way children do, we look at them coldly, so that they will calm down. What a hateful mirror those two faces were for me. They smiled the same way. Fortunately, kinship cannot be established on the basis of a smile. I went back to sit down next to Camille as calmly as possible, and pretended to laugh at the misadventures of poor Punch. I don't know if at that moment Camille could sense how terribly proprietary the grip of my hand on her little arm was.

*

At the end of the performance I put Camille in her pram and counted to ten. I knew that when I looked up Annie would be walking away; she would not linger, now that the object of her love was no longer in sight.

I had guessed correctly, this was not the first time she had hidden somewhere to be able to see Camille; her behaviour had betrayed the calmness and detachment of someone used to this sort of spying.

I had to follow her. Like the biter being bitten: I had to spy on the woman who was spying on me. I had to see where she went. With a bit of luck, find out where she lived, where she worked. Track her down, as if I were flushing out a dreaded illness, the source of which I had long been searching for – think of the relief it would bring.

But the further we went along the streets, the more I began to lose my nerve. Without a doubt, Annie was headed for my house. I hadn't been expecting it, I tried to think of a way to defend myself, I didn't want an argument in front of Camille. Then suddenly, at the crossroads to the street that led to my house I could no longer see her. At first I thought she had caught me out and had run away. And then something caught my eye along the unbroken façades: my gaze, hesitant and fascinated, froze at the sight of the huge lantern hanging over the Étoile du Berger.

A few metres ahead of me, on the same pavement, was what looked like an art gallery but was, in fact, a brothel.

I walked by. If everything had exploded at that moment, I would not have been surprised. I had just realised that Annie was working as a prostitute. Every passing gaze was levelled at me. Every finger pointed. Mouths twisted. The sounds around me changed. Stop, it's not me! She's the one who chose it. She could have decided to do something completely different. It's not me. It's life. I had nothing to do with it. She wanted to become a prostitute, that's her choice. Perhaps she has it in her blood – no, not in her blood, Camille, my God…In her body.

But my dejection and guilt did not last for long. As abruptly as I had tormented myself, I began to gloat wildly, relieved in a way I had never thought possible. This time it would be all over! Truly over. From where she now stood she could no longer harm me. She would never be able to take Camille from me. By profiting from her pride as a woman, she had forfeited her pride as a mother. Just let her try to come and claim my daughter – I'd know how to deal with her! I would tell her you cannot be a whore and a mother at the same time.

And while Paul might have gone off with a worker's daughter, he would never go off with a slut. What's more, a slut for the Boches. *Nur für Offizere.* The Étoile du Berger had been requisitioned.

How could she have stooped so low? Was it from all the time she spent lurking around my house? Or had she been drawn by the paintings in the window? Did she even know where she was going? That a shopgirl in her negligee would open the curtain? And why not? she must have thought on seeing her. She resigned herself to it. In order to stay near Camille, Louise, close by, and find shelter. It had been such a terrible winter. Eat all she liked. No need to dress up. And make the most of the coal, which must have been in plentiful supply for the clients.

Every day I made a sweep of the horizon and every day I saw her posted somewhere. Behind a tree, on a faraway bench, always with her eyes riveted on Camille. I had hesitated to go back to the Jardin des Champs-Elysées, but what was the point? No matter where I took Camille to play, in any park, she would find us, that I knew. Wherever I went she would follow. Leaving Paris wouldn't change anything, either. She would never take her eyes off Camille. And no town or village could protect me as well as Paris could. There are certain things that can exist only in capital cities, where problems can be masked, disabled, and where a nest of vipers can be smothered. I had to continue as I was, and not change a thing. If Annie had locked herself into prostitution, above all, I must not help her to get out of it by leaving.

I eventually got used to seeing her haunting the sphere of my life. Just as the German planes on patrol reminded me day and night that even the sky no longer belonged to us, Annie's lurking presence reminded me that my daughter did not belong outright to me. But Annie no longer made me afraid; in her situation she could risk nothing. We were like two enemies searching and not finding each other's Achilles' heel. In fact we shared the same Achilles' heel, and we could not make use of it, other than to ensure our own misfortune: it was Camille.

Before I found out that Annie was a prostitute, I didn't pay the slightest attention to the Germans. I walked by them haughtily; I watched as they opened our coffers and took everything; impassive and proud, I selected my friends and my social engagements carefully in the name of what I called honour and dignity. I was not in the Resistance, far from it, but I was extremely reluctant.

After I found out that Annie was a prostitute, I relented and went to their soirées: an exhibition by Arno Breker, a concert at the Palais de Chaillot, and I even organised dinners at home. I realise it was unacceptable but I was afraid that Annie might use her charms to win over a German officer and get Camille from me that way. I had to be able to defend myself in the event of such a ploy. I also needed protectors, acquaintances. I had to surrender, the better to fight back, if need be. For Camille's sake I went over to the enemy. But I would have done anything for Camille. How many nights did I wake up with my love for the child tight around my throat, so alive, so tenacious, that I could not get back to sleep?

Paul never understood, and I was never able to justify myself to him. At least, if he no longer loved me, I had provided him with a good excuse. His wife, the traitor. The collaborator. How could I have done that to him? While he was a prisoner. Did I not realise? Colluding with the enemy like that. The very people who had arrested Sophie. Did that not bother me either? Did the idea of betrayal never cross my mind?

How could he ask such a thing!

I looked him in the eye, coldly, ready to have it out, there and then. He wanted to talk about treason, then we would talk about treason. But he was circling round me, drunk with rage, obsessed with his own train of thought.

*

*

'So which one did you sleep with? Or maybe it should be which ones?'

How dare he? He was standing behind me; I whirled round and with the momentum, as if I were on a spring, unstoppable, I slapped him, so hard, so perfectly, so precisely that my hand reached its goal directly, as if all these years my body had been calculating the angle of the gesture so that it would reach its target with certainty and a brutal force.

Paul had come back on 20 August 1942. Camille had just turned two. I wasn't expecting him. The telephone rang. He was in Compiègne, his train had just arrived. The sound of his voice suddenly made no sense, nor did the desire to resume life with him by my side. La Relève, an initiative launched by Laval, had proved mostly ineffective, but it brought Paul back to me. One chance in a thousand; my bad luck, out of all those thousands. I hadn't been expecting it, for the most part it was only peasants who came back. I had come to terms with the idea of loving him in absentia, I often talked about him to Camille. A guardian figure who created a balance, the third angle of our triangle, absent, perfect, forgivable. But present: imperfect, unforgivable. After his return everything became complicated. Camille and I both wept a great deal, I because he had come back into my life, she because he had suddenly appeared in hers.

'Why is Papa here?'

'That's the way it is, sweetheart, a papa lives with his children, the way a maman does.'

'No. Maman's bed is mine. Papa go back to his war bed.'

*

236

*

It is so sweet to sleep with one's child, bodies so relaxed in the knowledge that that is all they have to do, sleep, and that there is no danger that they will have to submit to the onslaughts of a man. The onslaughts of a loyal husband, that is something one can abide, and even tell oneself sometimes how nice it is, but with an unfaithful husband one closes one's eyes and thinks how nice it would be just to sleep, or vomit, one hardly knows which.

Camille never let him go near her under any pretext. She would rush into my arms the moment she saw him. Paul would get terribly upset. She didn't want to go out for walks with him and when he left the house her little hand would tug on my skirt, full of hope:

'Has Papa gone back to the war?'

'No, darling, he'll be back tonight.'

'I liked Sophie better.'

I was worried. The danger had returned. For the time being Camille's rejection of her father suited my purposes, but she would eventually allow herself to be won over and everything would cheer up between the two of them. One day she would agree to go to the swings with him. And what would happen when Annie, from her hiding place, saw the two of them together? She would rush over to Paul, fall to her knees, beg him to believe her, Louise was her daughter, and Paul would say, 'Who is Louise?' and Annie would point to Camille swinging high, her legs bent back then stretched out, thinking that perhaps her papa was a nice man after all, he could push her closer to the sky than her maman could. And then Paul would think Annie was so beautiful, he wouldn't listen when she tried to

*

explain to him that she was working at the Étoile du Berger, all he could see was her smile, the same smile as Camille's, how had he failed to realise up to now, when it was so obvious? And they would go away together, the three of them, hand in hand.

And then there had been that dreadful evening. A few weeks after his return, Paul informed me, in his own way, that the past was not dead.

'I went to L'Escalier today. Jacques has kept it well-maintained: that was a good idea to ask him to stay there.'

Then I knew what was about to come. Before I even heard it, I could tell what it would be. Down to the very words.

'Have you had any news from Annie?'

So he had gone looking for her. With that name on his lips he would continue to go looking for her. He hadn't forgotten. The fact that this girl's body had been used by hundreds of German bodies would change nothing. The images from behind the curtains came back to me, the charm would be in full force. So, as if I were taking a child's costume out of an old trunk:

'She's married.'

I fed him my story about being a wartime godmother. It had discouraged one admirer, it would have to discourage this one, I had nothing else to fool him with, and to make him believe that she'd found love elsewhere seemed like the best way of loosening her grip. Only people who have no pride at all will go on clinging to a heart that has been taken, anyone else will give up, and Paul was a proud man. Then I got up and went into the bedroom.

✳

'Speaking of Annie, she asked me to give you this when you came back. I had completely forgotten.'

I handed him the pistol. For the first time I could tell that he was at a loss; for the first time he would have to come up with an excuse.

'My Derringer…I had lost it…wonderful! I wondered where it had got to. So it must have been…it must have been in the room without walls.'

'Yes, probably.'

He turned the little gun over and over in his hands, weighing the proof that Annie was gone from him. This hurt him; I could tell he was trying to understand what had happened. It hurt me, too, after all these years; it was not over, I still had to fight. They could run into each other anywhere, I could not control everything, and chance even less than the rest. Wherever I looked I was afraid. I was sorry I had not killed Annie.

All the more so because of the verdict that had been handed down. During the exodus from Paris there had been nurses who killed the patients they could not take with them. I had followed the story from the beginning. The nurses' lawyer spoke of the 'collective madness' that had gripped the country, a madness that in his view could, if not excuse, then at least explain their insane and criminal acts. And the judges had heeded his findings by granting attenuating circumstances, and giving the nurses – murderesses – nothing more than a suspended sentence. At that rate, I too should have administered a strong dose of morphine to Annie; it wouldn't have cost me anything, and now I would have some peace of mind. My God, peace of mind, that was all I aspired to, even if it meant forfeiting the pure

✳

peace of Christ and a guiltless conscience.

The noose was tightening with terrifying speed. A few days after that dinner, I received a call from a man I was paying to keep an eye on Louis. His colleague. A certain Maurice, a nice enough lad, but he needed money and he saw nothing wrong with telling me that today Annie had suddenly shown up again at the post office and that Louis seemed quite 'unsettled'.

'Thank you, I will send you your envelope poste restante. Let me know if they see one another again.'

This was no coincidence. Annie had something up her sleeve, you don't just suddenly show up like that for no good reason. Louis would find out that I had lied to him, that she wasn't married. They were going to come and take Camille from me.

The next morning I received another call.

'Good morning, Madame.'

'Yes?'

'Louis has broken up with his girlfriend, I thought you might be interested.'

'I pay you to find out whether your friend is seeing Annie, not to give me the most trivial details about him. Don't try to take advantage of me.'

I hung up on him.

So that's how it was? The moment that girl showed up somewhere, all the other girls were swept away. Was that what would happen to me, too, if Paul found her?

I waited. Despite the semblance of calm, I knew the situation was building to a climax, inexorably. I was no fool, this was the calm before the storm, the tempest. I had to find a way out. Every story needs resolution, that's just the way it is. I felt as if I were a sentry at a fortress, overwhelmed, running from one watchtower to another, north, south, east, west, trying not be caught out by the enemy. I always had to keep one step ahead.

'Hello?'

'Louis and your Annie had dinner together last night. They were rounded up after curfew but then were let go again this morning. They just left the house together after breakfast. Hello? Hello?'

'Yes, I'm here, but do be quick, I cannot spend hours on the telephone.'

'Annie lives at number 17, rue de Turenne. She's a shopgirl in a paint shop, and, tell you what, she's not half good-looking, that girl.'

'That is not information, merely your personal taste. Tell me instead what they did during the night.'

'I told you, time flies when you're having fun: they stayed out too late and were arrested after curfew.'

Untrue. I pictured them making their statement against me, telling the police everything. They would come and take Camille from me. I hung up. Perhaps I left my hand on the receiver for too long, I was staring at the Derringer, which had found its place again among the other weapons in the collection on the wall.

'Who was that?'

Paul was standing in the door. I turned round, quickly taking my hand from the telephone.

'No one.'

I could see that he didn't believe me. Never mind. I no longer had the time. I had to defend myself, they were going to come and take Camille from me. I ran to find my coat.

'Where are you going?'

✳

241

'Shopping.'

'But we were supposed to have lunch with the Pasteaus.'

'I'll be back by then.'

I left with Camille. I could not let myself be separated from her, anything but that.

I didn't understand. Annie did not live at 17, rue de Turenne. She lived at the Étoile du Berger. I had to make sure. Never mind if I gave myself away. Never mind if she recognised me, if someone described me to her – a woman with a little girl in her arms had been looking for her. Never mind if I met her face to face. The danger wasn't there, I could tell. I didn't have much time left to act, I could tell that too.

'I'm here to see Annie.'

A bleached blonde wearing furs had opened the curtain.

'Don't know no Annie.'

'Yes, a young girl who works here.'

'Thing is, there's only young girls what work here, you need to be more precise. That's a pretty kid you got there, if my mother'd known when I was that age what I'd turn into, she might've—'

I interrupted harshly.

'I know that Annie works here, she stole money from me, so either you call her at once, or I denounce her to Captain Schiller, who is a friend of mine, and I'm not sure that would be very good for the reputation of this house of yours, if one can even talk about a reputation where a brothel is concerned.'

'All right, all right, no need to go getting het up like that, ma'am. Can't do nothing about your money…

∗

as for Annie, I don't know where she is. Whether you believe me or not, she left yesterday without a word, left me no time to replace her. Can you imagine the fix she's put me in? How'm I supposed to deal with the regulars? They're so touchy, minute something goes wrong they take it personally. Already last night when I told them she wasn't here they looked at me with that suspicious way of theirs, the occupying forces doubting the good will of the occupied people. She's going to cause me trouble, that one, I can tell…Always the same thing, always the ones you least suspect who go and…'

I didn't wait to hear the rest. The game had begun, Annie was moving the pawns. Where had she found the courage to give it up? Why? For whom? Not for herself, at any rate, you never find that kind of courage for yourself. For Louis? Most likely. For Camille? I was sure of that too. They were going to come and take Camille from me.

I went to the address my informer had given me. 17, rue de Turenne. There was a little newsboy on the street corner. He had nothing to do, so I sent him to knock on every door in the building. My mission left him breathless: there was an elderly couple, the man opened the door, the old woman was sitting in an armchair, in a corner of the room there was a rabbit in a cage, it looked as old as they were, as if they had never been able to bring themselves to eat it. In the next apartment there was a mother with three children, he could only see two of them, they were drawing, but the third was calling out, he wanted the mum to come and wipe his bum. In another apartment there was no one, in any case, no one came to open the door. Then there was a grumpy fellow who looked like he was waiting for someone. That was on the third floor. Above that there was a pretty girl, all by herself...

'How old?'

'A little older than me. At any rate she had bigger tits than most girls my age. Very nice as well, she even bought a paper from me, that way I wouldn't have got the wrong door for nothing, she said nicely, and it would keep her busy until it was time to go to the gardens...'

'That's fine, thank you, here's something for you.'

'On the top floor, there was one more—'

'That's fine, that will do, you've told me what I wanted to know. Thank you, my boy.'

He was back at his spot on the corner of the street when I went over to him.

'I'll take a newspaper, too.'

How should I do it? I needed scissors and some glue. A bit further along the street I found a cobbler's, he was willing to lend them to me, but I had to be careful with the baby, they were leather scissors and very sharp. Thank you, monsieur, it's very kind of you...

But above all I had to be quick. Annie would be leaving for the gardens soon.

While waiting for the newsboy's report, I had hidden in the basement of the building. Ever since the first air-raids, the door had routinely been kept open. I went back there. At the cobbler's I had bought a little duck on wheels for Camille to play with, but of course she was more interested in what I was doing, and she stopped me from going as fast as I would have liked. But I managed to finish in time all the same.

I waited until I saw Annie leave the building. Once

✳

she had disappeared around the corner, I went up to the
fourth floor: the apartment on the left-hand side of the
landing, the newsboy had said. As I slipped the paper
under the door I prayed that the boy was not one of
those people who mix up left and right; my plan hung
by a thread. Like all plans.

I took a taxi. I only just had time to call by the
house. We had an appointment in the gardens half an
hour from then, but she didn't know that yet: a real
appointment this time.

'Go and show your duckie to Papa, sweetheart.'

'No.'

'Yes. You know, Papa knows how to make duckies
talk.'

'No, he doesn't make anyone talk. He doesn't even
talk himself.'

At home I changed my blouse and put on a black hat.
Paul was working in his study, and I set Camille and
her duck down on the sofa in front of him. I eyed the
Derringer on the wall, alongside the other weapons in
the collection.

'By the way, I won't be here for lunch. I'm going to
the cemetery. I can't take Camille, it's not the right place
for her.'

'Why on earth are you going to the cemetery now?
Can't it wait?'

'No, it cannot wait.'

'But how will I manage? She'll start crying.'

'If you don't put down your newspaper and play
with her a bit, yes, she will cry.'

Just then Camille interrupted us.

'Maman cut newspaper.'

✳

*

I was ill at ease.

'Papa, you want to cut newspaper, too? Please Papa?'

'No.'

I left the two of them, one screaming, the other mute and distraught. 'Maman cut newspaper.' Fortunately, she didn't yet have the words she needed to denounce me. The time during which one can keep things from children does not last long. Damn! I had forgotten to take a handkerchief.

I sat down on a bench and waited for Annie. She would come, I was sure of it. She would stand before me, pale and anxious at seeing me alone and dressed all in black.

It all happened just as I had imagined. She hurried over to me, and said tonelessly, 'Where is she? Where is Louise?'

I looked at her: could I do it? And I plunged ahead, coldly, disjointedly. The game had begun.

'Last night I left her in Paul's study, not long, just the time it took to go and fetch her a jumper...'

'Where is she?'

'...her hands had seemed cold, a child's hands at that age, they're often cold, even very cold. As I went down the stairs I called to her, but she didn't answer. I wasn't really worried, this often happens with children, when they hear you they don't always answer, it's the same thing even with adults...'

'Stop it, tell me where Louise is.'

'...she was lying on the floor, the little Derringer next to her. She must have taken it off the wall to play with it. Blood was pouring from her stomach...She's dead, Annie, Louise is dead. She must have pressed the

*

trigger and the bullet went straight into her stomach. I cannot understand how it happened, none of the weapons in the collection has ever been loaded. Ever.'

At that moment I looked up at Annie and saw she was having trouble absorbing what I had said. Her face resembled my lie, the blood had drained from her body. I don't know how many long seconds she stood there rigid in front of me. And then she screamed, the cry of a mortally wounded animal, and ran away.

I had no fear of bringing misfortune on Camille; it was Louise who had died.

What happened after that I can only imagine, but it must have gone just as I planned.

She went home. Some sorrows may dissolve in the street, or in a bar, but not the sorrow of a dead child. She could throw herself on her bed, or on the floor, or hide in a corner, but she had to get home.

17, rue de Turenne. Fourth floor, on the left.

Crossing the threshold she stepped on a sheet of paper. She lowered her eyes, instinctively, and she could not help but read it. I had not put the paper in an envelope; she would not have had the courage to open it. Nor had I folded it; she would not have had the courage to unfold it.

I had left her no choice but to read the letters I had cut out and glued to the sheet.

IT ISN'T NICE TO GO HIDING THINGS
WHO'S GOING TO TELL
YOUR NEW BOYFRIEND
THAT HE'S SLEEPING
WITH A WHORE

✳

*

She had not confessed to Louis, of that I am sure. You can tell the truth, the whole truth, when you are sure that you will never see someone again, but she did not want to lose Louis. The risk of the stain, the disgust that prostitution can inspire: not a risk you can take with a young man like Louis. He would not understand why she had compromised herself like that over the last two years. Only a 'mature' man can envisage helping a young woman out of such a situation, might even find a certain pleasure in it, the pathetic pleasure of withdrawing a prize from the reach of other men. A young boy has so many fresh, pure women at his disposal that he would no longer trade with someone like Annie.

Annie would be severely distressed by the letter. She would not think of me; I had not been a part of her life for years now. Letters of denunciation were so common in those days that anyone might be the author. A former client. A rival. One of Louis's jilted girlfriends. Vengeance was not mine alone.

A single argument might suffice to end it all with Louis. Perhaps it need not even be an argument, just an explanation. But she had just had tragic news, and she would be thinking in tragic terms. Louise was dead, and if Louis found out she was working as a prostitute he would never want anything to do with her again: that must be what she would say to herself.

I wanted to assail her from all sides, to stifle her. Through the people she loved. Destroy her radiant future, at the very moment when she had felt closer than ever to attaining it. I knew how propitious such

*

circumstances could be for sudden tragedy, for insanity. Like snatching a toy car or a doll from a child, the very toys you have just given them. Fury. Screaming. The end of the world. Louise. Louis. Everything collapsing, all at once.

She took care of the rest all on her own. She left her room, took her bicycle, pedalled all the way to Nuisement, and threw herself into the lake.

I only found out the following morning, when Jacques called me from L'Escalier to say that Annie had drowned; they had found her body.

I don't know who told him that – they never found her body. Village rumours are impenetrable, like the Chinese whispers that Camille used to like to play with me when she was a child; you never know at what point, or by whom, the truth has been distorted.

It was not that I had actually premeditated murdering her. I had to find a way to keep her out of my life for good, and quickly. I was going for broke. I knew her so well. I could hound her into a corner. Guess at every little convulsion of her soul that would eventually cause her to lose her footing and fall. Plot all the events, pile them on to break her. Overwhelm her, swamp her, with the worst things imaginable so that she could see no other way out, only death. Psychological manipulation is a weapon like any other, no more or less fallible, the only one, in any case, that can ensure a perfect crime. So perfect that even I was almost convinced I was not responsible for her death. In the end, perhaps I was right.

Just like soldiers going to war, my doubts only came later, as if the feeling of urgency had silenced all other

*

feelings, leaving room only for hard, efficient reason and action. My doubts came with time, with hindsight, with calm, and through the mirrors I gaze into like any other woman, but not for the same reasons. I often scrutinise myself, still astonished by my past deeds; before this I had never been capable of even a white lie of the most inoffensive sort. Perhaps I am like one of those repeat offenders of whom only good things are said, until they find themselves confronted once again with a similar situation and they commit a new murder. In certain specific circumstances a particular facet of the self comes to light, only to vanish again instantly the moment the circumstances change.

But when I speak of 'doubts', it stops there: I have never felt any remorse or guilt. I persist in thinking that Paul and Annie are the ones who drove me to do what I did. I have always thought that betrayal gives one every right.

I never told Paul that Annie had committed suicide. He would have wanted to believe it was for his sake, and their love affair would have become wonderful, romantic, eternal. His sorrow, too. I wanted that love affair to be trivial, vulgar, and common. Annie had gone off with someone else: that was all he was supposed to believe. And I would never inflict upon myself the worst enemy a woman can ever have: a dead woman, the woman you can always replace but never equal.

Paul never suspected the truth.

Nor did he suspect the truth about Camille, or if he did, he never spoke about it. And, as the years went by, he had to live with the terrible uneasiness of seeing the woman he had loved in his own daughter, visible,

*

invisible, like some aching ghost lurking where it should never have been. His mistress in his daughter, an unbearable combination.

But let there be no mistake, there were days when we did make up a fine family. A great many days, even. We too had our moments of deep, sincere joy, our contagious fits of laughter and gaiety.

And then there was Pierre's birth, a wonderful sunny spell in our life. Pierre is my son. Our son, Paul's and mine.

When I found out I was pregnant I hugged Camille as if she were the one who had made love to me, who had made this child. Her existence had so much to do with it, that I knew. Without her, Pierre would not exist, I am certain; like so many 'infertile' women I had conceived my little boy because I no longer expected him.

But there were also Paul's struggles, and his relapses. He was drinking.

I never wanted to admit to myself that it was all connected, but it was. He never forgot Annie. He was killed during the war in Indochina. The children suffered a great deal. And I did too, infinitely more than I would have expected.

These days, Camille has become a charming young woman, vivacious and passionate. Not always about life, but about her profession, definitely. She is a publisher. When she told me she was expecting a baby I wanted to believe that she was telling me about a new book.

But suddenly, after all these years only vaguely troubled by doubt, all my demons have awoken, instantaneously, violently unchanged.

I was foolish enough to believe that one could

*

extricate oneself from an act like mine.

The terrible fear of birth has started again, intact, raging.

I do not want to go through all that again. I'm too old, and suddenly my lie has taken on a new dimension. Until now it only concerned one person: Camille.

I never planned for my lie to outlive me. The nature of a lie is to be uncovered, unmasked, not to become a definitive, unshakable truth, beyond suspicion – the truth of lives as yet unlived, of people who will never have the means to know – I cannot uproot all those people yet to be born. To live in truth, people must know where they come from; when I see the point Camille has reached in her life, I am sure of that.

So, if something were to happen to me – and you will know, the day it does – I beg you to tell Camille everything: you are the only one who can. I know how difficult it might seem; think of it as my final wishes. I beg you. Tell her everything. Be honest. Even with the hardest truths, about the story, about me. Tell her about her mother, her mothers. And above all, don't bother to say kind things or words of comfort. Don't apologise, either for me or for you, you have nothing to blame yourself for, and in any case it would never be equal to her sorrow, or perhaps, even, her hatred. But do not worry, I am sure she will be all right, my daughter is strong. Unsinkable. Like her mother. And if she begins to founder, the child she is expecting will prevent her from going under, trust me. Tell her how much I love her, I beg you. Farewell, monsieur. Farewell, young man. And forgive me.

Everything was crystal clear, filthy, but crystal clear. Once she had finished her story, your mother got up and walked away. I watched her leave: she had the slow gait of someone who is overwhelmed, but at the same time she held herself upright, like those who know where they are going. She knew what she had to do, of that I am certain. That story was the very end of her life. There was nothing I could have done to stop her.

I worked like a dog all night, at my desk, filling the pages of this school exercise book in order to transcribe faithfully everything she had just told me. It was as if I had gone back in time, to those years when I would stand by my sorting table, memorising the compromising letters before I destroyed them, and when, at night, I would creep on my felt soles to the home of those to whom the letters had been addressed, in order to recite them.

Louis

I folded the sheet. I slammed the car door behind me and headed towards the church.

I had pictured it bigger. It was long, low, and narrow. All wood, like a cabin, except for the steeple, which was covered with tiles. It wasn't grand, but it was beautiful. I went closer.

There was music coming from inside. I would have preferred to be alone. I stood on the threshold: the softness of the light was calming, as were the rows of empty pews. I went in. A simple wooden rectangle: the nave, an apse, and neither side aisles nor upper floor. The statue of Saint Roch was there, standing under a stained-glass window. His trusted companion, the dog, was lifting the saint's cape to show his wound. There was water in the font. Cool water. I kept my fingers on my brow for a while before making a vague sign of the cross.

In front of me, next to the altar, a man was playing the organ. I could see him from the back, a priest. He wasn't wearing a cassock, but his white collar left no doubt, nor did the way he was playing, which seemed to me deeply religious. I took a few steps closer then withdrew again. I watched as the man let his fingers play over the keyboard: his broad neck, his thick grey hair. All of a sudden, I knew who he was.

And I recognised the scent from the letters: the woody smell of incense that I had not been able to identify.

And from the 'Hours of Confession' handwritten on a sheet stuck to the heavy wooden door, I recognised that capital 'R' amidst the other lowercase letters, that handwriting that had turned my life upside down.

It was him all right. Louis.

His arms suddenly froze on the keyboard, the music stopped. Had he sensed that someone was watching him? I left the church. Did he turn around? I started the car.

Louis had taken such care to keep me from finding him, I would not go against his wishes, not now that I knew everything.

'Everything was as it should be,' he had said, years before, when, in this very same church, he fell in love with Annie, also seen from behind. Louis deserved to be left in peace. By inflicting her confession upon him, Maman had forced him to go back into his memories; I would not revive them by introducing myself. I would not impose on him any physical resemblance to that woman he had loved so much.

I watched as the church faded behind me in the rear-view mirror, that church where Maman had come to ease her conscience and find a messenger. The notebook was open on the seat next to me. Louis' handwriting, with Maman's words. Merciless. I could feel the steering wheel brush against my belly, my baby. My mother had killed for me; she had killed herself for him. She had the slow gait of someone who is overwhelmed, but at the same time she held herself upright, like those who know where they are going. She knew what she had to do.' Maman knew that she would accelerate in the bend and that she would not brake. It was bound to be the bend where her own parents had died; that road was not one of her usual routes. In the end, Maman had acted like Papa. How many people commit suicide that way in 'an accident' in order to spare their loved ones the guilt?

I took the road that went along the lake, the water stretching as far as the eye could see. I could not stop thinking of Annie's body lying somewhere at the bottom. Tears were streaming down my cheeks. I stopped the car. I reread the notebook, choking on every word. Pierre my brother, you will go on saying I was Maman's favourite – if only you knew how I would rather have been her daughter. The lake water sparkled with the reflection of the sky. Suddenly a dark cloud moved over the surface of the water. I looked up from the notebook. The Lady of the Lake, holding Annie at arm's length, to give her back to me? No, a flight of cranes. Thousands, perhaps, as if all the oracles in the world had concentrated over my head. They flew in procession across the sky, a majestic choreography of birds, without a choreographer. I too was a migrating bird, I had been made to migrate from my mother. Maman, why didn't you keep me with you?

A little aeroplane was approaching the spot where I had parked. It was landing. I wanted nothing more to do with the earth. The sky was what I needed right now, that sky where all my loved ones now lived. I went over to the flying club. The pilot welcomed me. Quarter of an hour? Half an hour? – An hour. I could not have dreamed of a better guide, he knew the lake like the back of his hand. 'Fantastic,' I said as he helped me climb in. Seven months, I'd be okay, no risk I'd give birth up there. It would probably be a boy. A future pilot! Maybe...

I watched the water recede below us. It was magnificent, immense and magnificent. I felt so alone. I wouldn't make it. The pilot was talking through my headphones, extending his arm to show the sights: the church at Nuisement, last remnant of the timber-frame churches...I knew the story, thanks.

'Look at the light!' The pilot pointed to the sky with its fiery sunset colours. The aeroplane was gaining in altitude. I let the headphones slide onto my shoulders; I didn't want to listen to him any more. I held the notebook tight. My baby was moving a lot, I ran my hand over my belly to reassure it. The aeroplane kept climbing, the words were dancing, coming together, and slowly everything was becoming clear. Look at the light.

I was born from a father
who went to war
leaving behind him
a little pistol for my pocket
if I was a boy
and two women whom he loved
each one in his own way
two women
who didn't know yet
that I would exist
only he knew
I exist because of love
I exist because of hate
I was born from a father who went to war

Paul said
'So be it!
If to be a husband worthy of the name
you think I have to sleep with that girl
then I shall do it…
but only once, you understand?'

Paul knew what he had to do
on the date they'd agreed on, he came home early
from the office
in the drawing room wasting no time
'let's go!'
no time to look at Elisabeth
no room for procrastination
he didn't turn round
never doubting for a moment that Annie would follow

he went first into the room without walls
no time for chivalry here
in front of him
between the easels and the strong smell of paint
a bed
he looks away, blinking rapidly
he goes over to the heavy curtain opposite him
pulls it aside and opens the window behind it
to let in some air

he plants himself there
the way he always plants himself
in front of the fireplace in the drawing room
something he liked to do, to stand there
it's in his nature, Paul's nature
suddenly the white muslin, the double curtain
slips through the window and flutters gently
caught at the top
Paul's eyes staring
and he is speaking
but he is aggressive
he is beside himself, with this situation
this girl above all
who put this idea into Elisabeth's head

I don't know what you are expecting
but nothing will happen between us
we will stay here a few minutes
and then I will go out
you will wait before you follow me
enough time to tidy yourself up

a leaden silence fell in the room
the only lightness from the curtain
fluttering before Paul's eyes

after a few minutes had gone by
Paul headed to the door to leave
before he turned round, spiteful
uttering a few threats
to prevent Annie from telling Elisabeth everything

Paul closed the door behind him
and went back into the drawing room
to stand by the fireplace
his spot, summer and winter alike

Elisabeth looked at him
the way you look at a traitor who is loyal to his habits
without ever thinking for a moment
that if he was loyal to any habit
it was to her
it was 9 April
the andirons were empty
the sun was warm outside

on 9 May, Paul, who was counting the days,
announced to Elisabeth that Annie was not pregnant
he thought he could leave it there,
not have to add anything
he was not expecting questions

'how do you know?'

Paul was troubled for a moment
seeing himself for a moment again in the room without
walls
standing by the curtain as it fluttered, fluttered
fluttered

'If Annie was not pregnant
she would wedge the curtain of the room
in the window
that way, in the evening, as I came down the drive
I would see the curtain hanging outside
and then I would know and could tell you
we decided together
after we…well, you know…
once we had finished'

Paul was lying
he had just made up the code
the complicity
to explain how he knew
that Annie was not pregnant

if she had not been so upset by the news
Elisabeth would have noticed that morning
that Paul was not standing in front of the fireplace
the way he normally did
but that he was standing by the window

Elisabeth would have understood that
from that spot, not his usual spot
Paul was watching out for Annie
as she came up the drive
to stop her in the hall

and tell her about the curtain
so she would not betray them

'I told Elisabeth you aren't pregnant
I told her about the curtain
that you had wedged it in the window
to let me know'

Paul might have grabbed Annie by the arm
to hold her back
miming so that she would understand
but Annie freed herself
waiting in the hall no longer
than any other morning
always his despicable familiarity with her
his nasty arrogance
Annie could not stand this man
but she already knew that Elisabeth would not give up
she knew his wife better than he did
so, speaking with the greatest composure

'I agree
I agree to go on trying
until we manage it'

to contradict that boor
let them meet again
put that bully in his place
she'd act familiar with him too
Paul was aghast at her effrontery
his eyes blinking rapidly
he went out

if Paul knew that Annie was not pregnant
it was not because of some curtain
it was simply that nothing had happened
that first time between them
in the room without walls
but love and clear-sightedness never go together
and Elisabeth always believed the opposite

thanks to what gesture?
what word?
what silence?
did Paul and Annie feel their desire
they alone know
the moment they began to love
the moment Paul's lie finally became the truth
and the white muslin curtain, their code
their complicity

when she spied on those lovers
with their unfruitful coupling
Elisabeth never acknowledged their low-spoken words
her rage that she could not grasp them
hid the most important thing from her
their murmuring, alone
troubled and suspicious
why did they need to speak so low?
they were alone, supposedly

Elisabeth should have understood
that invisible proof
of meetings she did not suspect
the habit of whispering

that the lovers had kept from their other trysts
trysts on other days of the week
because the Saturdays were not enough
trysts when they were not alone
when Elisabeth too was at L'Escalier

when in the evening as he came down the drive
the curtain in the room without walls was caught in the
window
and fluttered lightly
in the outside air
it was a sign that tonight
the mistress would wait for her lover

look at the light

'Louis pedalled furiously
the lake was only a few hundred metres away
as he went by L'Escalier
he slowed down, instinctively
looking for Annie's bicycle somewhere
leaning against a wall
but there was no sign of life
only the curtain in one room
fluttering
caught in the French doors
like a ghost'

nothing but the curtain in a room
fluttering
caught in the French doors
a sign that the mistress was waiting for her lover

Annie was not dead

Paper-scissors-stone
WATER
Annie's body never surfaced

Annie was not dead

but Jacques told Elisabeth
that they had found her body

village rumours are impenetrable
one never knows who causes the truth to be distorted
Elisabeth should have guessed

Jacques, busy setting a few traps
for hares, perhaps, or chopping wood
saw Annie approach the lake
throw her bicycle to the ground
fill her pockets with stones
and lower herself in the water
at the most dangerous spot

he ran faster
than his dead leg would allow
he jumped into the muddy water
he couldn't see her any more
finally after long minutes had passed
he felt Annie's body in his hands
heavy with stones
he took her out

and carried her to L'Escalier
Annie was raving
she said it again and again
so Jacques did what she asked
despite the cold
open the window
open the window
open the window
and the curtain began to flutter as in the time of love
where the mistress waited for her lover

Annie was not dead
and Elisabeth found out, one day
at the foot of the steps to my apartment
she turned pale
that figure in the courtyard

she would have recognised her anywhere
when she came up she squeezed my arm, hard
it was no longer as small as in the puppet show days
unsinkable like her mother
Elisabeth was right
there was no point going to a different park
Annie would never have let her daughter out of sight

she had given up her role as mother
she would claim that of grandmother
the baby's birth would blow everything sky high
Elisabeth knew this
she no longer had the strength to fight
disappear and make room
that was all she had left

Annie had never let her daughter out of sight
from behind the pane
she waved goodbye
as the curtain fluttered closed
I thought
of how the last survivor of a family
never receives any letters of condolence

Annie had never let her daughter out of sight
from behind the window of her loge
she said goodbye
my mother didn't die
she would give me back my jumper that night

look at the light

ACKNOWLEDGEMENTS

This book would never have existed without my love, without my child. Without my love, who watched me work in silence and then, when the time came, became an exceptional reader. Without my child, who came into my life when I needed him.

This book would never have existed without my parents, who always gave me their full support, all the more remarkable given the fact that the profession of writer is not exactly a profession in their eyes.

Without my brother, for a very special conversation on the terrace.

Without my friends who, year after year, never stopped asking, 'How are you getting on with your novel?'

Without Barnabé who, one evening, asked me to tell him the story.

Without Vanille, always so considerate.

Without Ludy, without Elsie, who have enabled me to work with my mind at rest.

My thanks to Laurent Theis, François George and Bruno Gaudichon for being such gifted history teachers.

My thanks also to Olivier Orban and Isabelle Laffont for welcoming me into their publishing houses. And thank you to Muriel Beyer for her advice.

But above all, this book would never have existed without Charlotte Liebert-Hellman who had the faith, and the wisdom, before anyone else, to set off with me, down this road.